CW01202327

Frank Clark

Our Vacations

Frank Clark

Our Vacations

Reprint of the original, first published in 1874.

1st Edition 2024 | ISBN: 978-3-36884-591-9

Verlag (Publisher): Outlook Verlag GmbH, Zeilweg 44, 60439 Frankfurt, Deutschland
Vertretungsberechtigt (Authorized to represent): E. Roepke, Zeilweg 44, 60439 Frankfurt, Deutschland
Druck (Print): Books on Demand GmbH, In de Tarpen 42, 22848 Norderstedt, Deutschland

OUR VACATIONS:

WHERE TO GO,

HOW TO GO,

AND HOW TO ENJOY THEM.

By FRANK E. CLARK.

BOSTON:
ESTES AND LAURIAT,
143 WASHINGTON STREET.

Entered, according to Act of Congress, in the year 1874,
BY ESTES AND LAURIAT,
In the Office of the Librarian of Congress, at Washington.

Stereotyped at the Boston Stereotype Foundry,
19 Spring Lane.

TO MY CLASSMATES,

T. E. C., S. W. A., AND *L. H. R.,*

WITH WHOM I HAVE SPENT SOME OF THE PLEASANTEST
OF VACATION WEEKS,

This Little Volume is Inscribed

BY ONE OF THE "QUARTETTE."

CONTENTS.

CHAPTER	PAGE
I. Preliminary.	9
II. To the White Mountains for Fifteen Dollars.	14
III. To Canada. — Montreal. — Quebec. — Ottawa. — River St. Lawrence.	57
IV. The Tent on the Beach.	115
V. Down East. — St. John. — Prince Edward Island. — Cape Breton. — Halifax.	149

Our Vacations:

HOW TO ENJOY THEM.

OUR VACATIONS,

AND

HOW TO ENJOY THEM.

CHAPTER I.

If the reader were entitled to know the whole truth, we should confess to a few conscientious qualms for not consigning this opening chapter to that sepulchre for an author's good wishes, trembling hopes, and unnecessary explanations, called an introduction or preface.

For, indulgent reader (this phrase is introduced on information, before commencing our book, that this was the proper way to address you), instead of getting a sniff of the sea in the very first page, or diving into the heart of the Adirondacks with the opening sentence, we are obliged to place before you a very few introductory pages of explanation, which are not labelled " introduction " for the very good reason that we wish to have them read — a piece of good fortune which is supposed to fall to the lot of but few prefaces.

But if these first pages were not read, we should have visions of many scornful noses turned up at this little book, and, in imagination, hear many sarcastic remarks, such as, " Walk to the White Mountains indeed! A pretty way of travelling this man recommends! To Canada for fifty dollars! Ridiculous! He must mean one hundred and fifty dollars." Yet we do not mean one hundred and fifty dollars, for, leave off the first three words, and with that sum in your pockets you can start from Boston and see all the sights of the Canadas in a two weeks' vacation trip. Moreover, we will tell you how the White Hills, the Mecca of wearied, city-worn pilgrims, may be reached, and a delightful vacation of three weeks spent among them for fifteen dollars; and for as many dollars as it takes to spend a single day at a first class sea-side hotel, we will tell you how you can live a week at the sea-shore in a far more enjoyable way.

So, friend of the plethoric purse, we would advise you to read no farther, unless, indeed, Newport, and Saratoga, and Long Branch have become utterly wearisome, and you have a notion of trying a poor man's vacation just as you would take a glass of soda " plain " after having " made a night of it."

But this little book is written for the great middle class, to which so many of us must necessarily belong — for the city clerk who gets his ten, fifteen, or twenty dollars a week, who looks with longing eyes from the hot, red bricks to the cool, green country, but who yet always sees an inseparable connection between the green fields and forests and greenbacks; for the country minister who longs to get away from his little parish into fresh scenes, where the croakings of brother A and the complaints of widow B will fail to reach him; for the doctor who has had plenty of patience, but very few patients; for the briefless barrister; in short, for any one in whose slender salary the bills of the butcher, and baker, and candlestick-maker leave such a narrow margin at the end of the year, that he finds the doors of our fashionable watering-places barred against him as really as though they were the very gates to the garden of Eden. In other respects than extreme exclusiveness, we imagine that the modern hotel resembles the ancient Paradise but little. The fig leaf has certainly been very much expanded since the days of Mother Eve, and Father Adam's *cuisine* differed considerably from the *table d'hôte* of a fashionable watering-place hotel. Indeed, we flatter ourselves that in visiting the mountains and sea-shore, as we are about to relate, we come much nearer to the customs of Paradise than do those who pay five dollars per day for the privilege of existing at the Crawford House or Congress Hall. However this may be, the reader may be assured that these vacation trips have actually been made by the writer in the way and for the sum mentioned, and can be taken again by a thousand others.

Especial pains have been taken that the statements of expenses, and the description of routes, outfits, &c., should be accurate and trustworthy; and our hope is, that many work-worn souls, who otherwise could not take a summer vacation, by following the example of Tom, Dick, and Sam, may gain inspiration from a few weeks spent among the hills or upon the seashore, that will carry them more happily through another twelvemonth of care and toil.

CHAPTER II.

TO THE WHITE MOUNTAINS FOR FIFTEEN DOLLARS.

Now, don't mentally consign us to an insane asylum, kind reader, when you glance at the above caption, and score off on your fingers — " Railroad fare twenty dollars, hotel bills forty dollars, carriage hire fifteen dollars, sundries twenty dollars;" for on our trip to the mountains we mean to have no railroad fares, or hotel bills, or carriage hire to pay.

" How shall we go, then?" do you inquire.

Why, by the turnpike, and on our own good legs, to be sure; for what other purpose, pray, were legs and turnpikes made?

One would think, from the antipathy which some people show to using their locomotive powers, that they were only meant for the tailor to exercise his skill upon, and that highways were intended solely for quadrupeds.

Well, having made sure that the means of getting to the mountains are both inexpensive and always at our command, the next thing we want to secure is, a party of five or six good fellows, just like ourselves — Tom, who is "such a good hand at a story;" and Dick, who is so good natured; and Sam, who is one of the best hearted fellows in the world; and Hiram and Jack — you know whom I mean; — but the grumbler and fault-finder must certainly be left out of our party.

Nothing would go right if he were with us. The coffee would always be muddy, the roads would be sure to be "confoundedly dusty," and the villages "wretched little hamlets." Mount Washington would surely be enveloped in a cloud when he made the ascent, and the "Old Man of the Mountain" would scowl more fiercely than ever when he gazed at him. Yes, our grumbling friend must be left at home, by all means.

Should any of our lady friends read this book, let them not feel excluded from our party if they have a desire for the muscle and happiness of the cliff-climber.

Let it be understood, too, that, wherever in these pages the masculine pronoun occurs in reference to the travellers, the feminine is included, as in law the word man means woman also. For this vacation trip is quite as practicable for a lady of reasonably strong constitution as for the Tom, Dick, Sam, and Hiram before alluded to.

Indeed, we have before us now an account of such a trip to the mountains, taken by a party of young ladies from Portland, at less expense than the jaunt we are about to describe; and a most delightful expedition it was, if we may judge from their account of "How we did it."

To be sure, a party which is partially made up of ladies may not be able to make quite as long daily marches as one in which the fair sex is wholly wanting; but this difficulty can easily be remedied by spending more days upon the road, which, perhaps, would be fully as agreeable to all parties as a more hurried journey.

Now that the party is made up, the next thing will be our outfit.

And first we must get a horse and wagon. Our steed need not be a Bucephalus, by any means. A strong, trustworthy animal, who knows a piece of white paper from a ghost, and can pick up his dinner from the road-side without whinnying for oats or corn meal for desert, is more serviceable to us among the New Hampshire hills, than a Dexter or a Longfellow would be.

Such a horse we can easily hire for a dollar a day, while the wagon body he is to draw ought not to cost us more than five dollars for the trip. This wagon is to carry our tent, provisions, and blankets; and for this purpose an ordinary express wagon, covered with a canvas top, well painted to keep out the rain, answers as well as anything.

It is very amusing to see what mistakes this nondescript vehicle of ours will give rise to when we get into the backwoods settlements. From one house a woman will rush in post-haste, and cry out at the top of her lungs, that she wants two pounds of beefsteak. We politely explain that we do not run a meat cart, and drive on a mile farther, to the next farm-house. From this we see a small boy emerge, waving violently a red flag. This is evidently meant to attract our attention, but whether to give us notice of an auction or a case of small-pox within, we are at a loss to determine, until we discover that we are mistaken for the baker, as the boy bawls out, "Ma wants a brick loaf of bread." At the next little collection of houses, half a score of children will gather around us, with eager inquiries as to where the next show will be, evidently mistaking us for the advanced guard of some "world-renowned circus." Thus on all the roads among the mountains, which are a little off the regular routes of pleasure travel, our strange team will be almost as rare a sight as a new comet, and will afford a fruitful topic of conversation for days after we have passed.

But to return to our outfit.

The first thing to go into the wagon will be an A tent, large enough to hold our party. For this R. M. Yale, or any dealer in tents, will probably charge us at least three dollars per week; but if we happen to know of some friend or charitably disposed person who has an unused tent on hand, we can get it, very likely, for a third of that sum. Such an exorbitant rent is asked for these canvas houses, that a few weeks of camp life would cover their first cost, so that it would be cheaper, in most cases, to buy the tent outright, and sell it again at the end of the trip. But there is generally little need of paying this price.

The tree poles of the tent should ride on the bottom of the wagon, with the canvas over them; and though they will stick out behind in a rather awkward manner, they will be found convenient to hang our lantern and tin pails upon, if the wagon is very full. Then in the front part of the wagon will come the barrel of hardtack — Pilot A if our teeth are strong and our digestion good, though a softer and richer variety can be had at a higher price, should we desire it.

We shall find that one barrel of pilot bread will just about last a party of half a dozen for three weeks. Next will come one keg of pickles, an indispensable article if any of the gentler sex are to accompany us, and in any case a great addition to the ham and hard tack, which often, when encamped away from villages and farm-houses, we shall be obliged to make the staple of our meals.

Beside the pickle keg will fit in nicely a box of hams, coffee, sugar, condensed milk, corn meal, salt pork, cheese, salt, and pepper. These are all the varieties of provisions that it is really necessary to take on an expedition of any length; and if one or two of these articles, even, were left behind, it would be no serious loss. Of course it is expected that much of our food will be bought on the way; but of such staple articles as coffee, sugar, and pilot bread, it is both cheaper and more convenient to keep a supply on hand.

Two medium-sized hams will be enough for our party, we shall probably find, while we shall need at least five pounds of coffee, and twenty pounds of sugar to sweeten it.

Nothing is more essential to camp life than the coffee-pot. Its fragrance as it bubbles on the stove, before supper, is enough to make the crustiest nature genial, and its aromatic flavor will encourage and strengthen us for a hard day's tramp, or will soothe and dissipate the aches and stiffness of a twenty mile walk, as nothing else in our larder will do. Long may the coffee-bag hold out, say we.

Of course we want the salt pork (five or six pounds of it), to use in cooking the speckled trout, which we have already caught in imagination, a hundred times over, from the mountain streams.

The corn meal will be useful to roll our fish in before frying them, as well as to make the Johnnie cakes, which, as an alternate with our hard tack, will seem so delicious to our hungry souls. Borden's condensed milk makes a very good and convenient substitute for milk in coffee, though it is worth little for other purposes.

As for prepared meats, we had better not take many cans of them, unless we have a notion of treating the New Hampshire crows and hawks to their contents. The picture of the sirloin roast on the outside of the can looks very juicy, to be sure, and the labels, " Roast Beef," and " Chicken Soup," sound extremely inviting. But, alas, we can hardly make a meal of the name or picture, and upon opening our can of " Roast Beef," we shall find nothing but a square chunk of " Mystery," and a very tasteless chunk it will be too; while the " Chicken Soup " (we are fortunately told what it is in plain print, on the outside) will hardly be appreciated, unless one has a decided liking for hard little cubes of carrot and turnip.

If an apology is required for the minuteness with which the contents of our provision-box are catalogued, it is humbly submitted that repeated experience shows that the articles mentioned are, on the whole, the best for a jaunt like ours.

Next, we shall put into our wagon a box containing our coffee-pot, spider, and small iron kettle, besides the tin plate, cup, knife, fork, and spoon for each one of the party.

On top of all these boxes we can pile our rolls of blankets, one or two for each man, not forgetting a couple of rubber blankets to spread on the floor of the tent; and last of all will come our stove, which should be small and light, weighing not more than forty pounds (such a one as can be bought at almost any old iron store for a dollar and a half). The little stove will be found a great convenience, for it is easily handled by one man, and saves the great bother of always having a fireplace to build when a cup of coffee or a slice of fried bacon is wanted.

Now the wagon is all snugly packed, and, having donned our very oldest and coarsest clothes, we shall be ready to start at daybreak to-morrow for the White Hills. A very good uniform, by the way, for such a pedestrian tour, is a blue flannel shirt, and stout gray trousers, without coat or vest, though it would be well to put coats in the wagon, to provide for the contingency that the nights among the mountains may be cool.

Fifteen miles will be enough for the first day's march (we shall all agree on this point before the day is over, I am sure), and if we start by six o'clock, or as soon as we have surrounded a good hot breakfast, we shall have made our fifteen miles before two o'clock in the afternoon. And O, the delights of those long summer afternoons in camp!

Tom, and Hiram, and Jack, perhaps have done their share of the afternoon's work in putting up the tent, and arranging things inside; while it is for Dick and Sam to superintend the dinner.

How fragrant that whiff of coffee was that just now floated into the open tent! How cheerily the fire crackles in the stove, and the bacon sizzles in the spider!

How those pains and aches, which the fifteen miles of steady tramping put into our legs, ooze out of them, as we stretch ourselves at full length, in Oriental fashion, upon the blankets! In short, what a jolly time we are having, and what a grand thing tent life is after the day's work is done!

And now Dick is pounding on the kettle by way of a gong, to let us know that dinner is ready. Did any one ever taste such crisp ham and fried potatoes? The pilot bread is a little hard, to be sure, but then it is wonderfully sweet — isn't it? Surely hens never laid such fresh eggs in the region of Boston! Indeed, how could anything be changed for the better?

Even this barren, old New Hampshire pasture, which stretches in front of us, looks almost glorified as we view it through the delicious steam that arises from our coffee-cup. By and by it begins to grow dark; we have thought best to "turn in" early, and nothing is now to be seen in the tent but six long mummies rolled in blankets.

Soon the last story has been told, the last conundrum "given up," the last joke cracked, the soughing of the wind in the pine branches above us grows more and more indistinct — and — Well, it is morning, and Tom is stirring about the tent, trying to impress on four desperately sleepy individuals that it is time to be getting breakfast.

It is wonderful how completely the roseate hue which surrounded everything yesterday afternoon has departed.

The pasture in which the tent is pitched *is* a wretched rocky field, after all. It seems as though the damp wood never would burn, and when it does, the spider full of ham, which is to make our breakfast, will be sure to burn with it. And then we all feel so stiff, and sore, and uncomfortable generally, that we are a good-natured party, indeed, if we get through the morning without any exhibitions of total depravity. But a generous cup of coffee will dispel many of these evil spirits of ill-nature; and a couple of miles of walking will limber up our locomotive powers, and drive away the rest of them, so that, long before the sun is two hours high, you couldn't find a jollier set of fellows than are we.

But here we are on the second day of our trip, and we haven't yet told the reader that we started with him from the beautiful little village of Center Harbor, New Hampshire. If you are Hubbites, in order to join us you must trudge through North-eastern Massachusetts, and South-eastern New Hampshire, along the eastern shore of charming Winnepiseogee, until, at about the end of the fourth day out, you will find yourselves encamped at Center Harbor. If it is not your good fortune to reside in the Trimountain city, you will doubtless take some other route; but, at any rate, you will be very likely to pass through Center Harbor; so we will follow the ramblings of our mountaineers from this point.

Some spot in the neighborhood of Tamworth will be our camping-ground on the first night out from Center Harbor, after a pleasant day's walk of seventeen miles. And now we begin to get into the midst of the grandest mountain scenery. Beyond the village of Tamworth looms up Chicorua (Coroway in the vernacular of the inhabitants), and a most remarkable mountain it is. No other hills are in its immediate neighborhood to lessen its effect, while its precipitous sides form almost a perfect cone, whose apex is so pointed, that only a few persons can stand upon it at the same time. The Tamworthians have a legend to the effect that the mountain takes its name from an Indian chief, who, after murdering a family of white men, unwisely took refuge on this mountain. Here he was pursued by the avenging whites, and, on the very top, surrounded by his enemies, with no way to escape, was killed in a manner that fully satisfies the demands of poetic justice, and that affords a thrilling plot for the imagination of any dime novel writer in the country.

A day devoted to visiting "Coroway" and the beautiful lake which lies at its base will be well spent if we can afford the time; but if not, we must push on the next day to North Conway, twenty miles farther into the mountains than our last camp. This we shall find a beautiful place, full of boarding-houses, and a very high place to live in, in every sense of the word. Hitherto we have been able to buy all the eggs we wanted for fifteen or twenty cents a dozen, but here they make a sudden leap to thirty cents. The cows, too, will only give milk for eight cents a quart at Conway, though in other towns we have had to pay but half that price; so that, in order to live within our fifteen dollars, we shall be obliged to draw largely on the hard tack barrel. Indeed, we shall find that the price of living will continue to rise as we ascend.

It is thought by some that the people of this region charge a dollar for every foot they get above the level of the sea; thus at Conway you could spend the season at a fashionable hotel for two or three thousand dollars. At the Crawford, farther up, the expenses would probably not be more than four thousand; while at the Tip-top House, which is something more than six thousand feet high, you could get along very comfortably for six thousand dollars. We give no voucher for the exact truth of this statement; it is only approximate.

At Conway we shall find a very good place to pitch our tent, in a pine grove, a little east of the village, and, as the next day's march will take us out of the bounds of civilization, it will be well for us to have Conway's excellent artist take a picture of our party in camp, should we desire a more permanent impression of the way we looked " the summer we went to the mountains " than our memories will be likely to retain.

Of course Conway, like all these mountain towns, has innumerable cascades, and chasms, and mountain views, to show the astonished traveller; but unless we have plenty of time at our disposal, we shall be likely to push on, the next day, in the direction of Bartlett.

It is often amusing to notice the different answers we shall get to the frequent question, "How far," to a place ten miles or more away. "Good morning, my friend," we will say to a farmer, who is busily hoeing his paternal potato patch: "how far is it to Bartlett?" "Wal, I reckon it's nigh onto seventeen mile," he will answer; and we pass on, congratulating ourselves that we have got an easy day's march before us. Soon we pass an Irishman working on the road, and propound to him the same question. " Sure an' it's twenty shar-rp miles," he will be very likely to reply. A tourist, perhaps, will be the next person we meet. "How far to Bartlett? O, a deuce of a ways; twenty-five miles at least." By this time we shall probably give up inquiring, and come to the conclusion that Bartlett is a Jack-o'lantern, which retreats as we advance, while very likely we shall find at night, when we have caught the fugitive, and pitched our tent in the very midst of her, that none of our informants came within a league of the correct distance.

Not that Bartlett is anything like a score of miles from our camp at North Conway; if we follow our usual custom of doing the principal part of our walking early in the day, we shall pass through this pretty little mountain village about the time that the early worm is popularly supposed to be devoured, and shall get quite a distance into the ungranted lands of New Hampshire before the afternoon sun tells us it is time to pitch our tent.

And these ungranted lands, it may be taken for granted, will never find anybody willing to take a grant of them, for agricultural purposes at least, so rough and rocky are they. Indeed, you might as well try to cultivate the slate roof of a meeting-house. A mansard roof, with a covering of asbestos, would be a far more desirable location.

But the more ungrantable the country becomes, the higher do the mountains tower on every side; and thus the law of compensation equalizes things, making the scenery grander and more picturesque as the country becomes more uncivilized and the roads more impassable.

It is something above thirty miles from North Conway to the place we shall make our headquarters during our stay among the White Hills, — rather a long day's march over the rough mountain roads, — and we shall probably be ready to encamp by the time we get to the Crawford House, some eighteen or twenty miles from our last camp.

All the land in this neighborhood, for eighteen miles on either side of the road, is owned by an eccentric old gentleman named Beamis, who has built a very pretty cottage near the old Crawford House.

It is whispered that Dr. Beamis is rather opposed to having parties encamp upon his ground; but we shall find plenty of room for our tent beside the public road, without trespassing upon the doctor's eighteen miles of wilderness.

Three miles from this camp is the Willey House, a place which the standard reading book of thirty years ago impressed so strongly upon the children of the last generation. And a tolerably correct picture the old reading book gives of this historic house, even at the present day, barring, of course, the family, whom, if memory serves, the artist represents fleeing in dire dismay, as well they might, some in one direction and some in another, from the approaching avalanche.

On a former visit to the mountains we saw a girl standing in the doorway of this very house, who certainly would have been safe had she belonged to the original Willey family, for surely nothing would have aroused her stupid, lethargic soul to attempt a flight. As we approached the house, we very naturally asked her,—

"Is this the old Willey House?"

"Dunno," was the laconic answer we received.

"What, don't you know whether this was the house that so wonderfully escaped destruction in the avalanche of 1826, when all the family, who attempted to escape, were killed?"

"Dunno," she again replied.

And "Dunno," was all we could get from this sapient damsel; and we had to seek for our desired information elsewhere.

It is curious to notice the different varieties of character one meets on a trip like ours. In the first place, we shall find quite a number like the girl just alluded to. To this class belong the crusty old farmers, who have lived half a century within sight of the grandest mountains of New England, yet who have never seen the glorious view from their top, because, forsooth, they regard every day as wasted that is not spent grubbing in their corn-field or potato-patch. These men would hardly know it, should the judgment day begin upon earth, and would be very likely to mistake Gabriel's trumpet for a fish-horn.

Then there is another species of the *genus homo* yclept Yankee, often met, who are just the opposite of these. Such men are not only ready to impart a vast amount of information and advice, but are exceedingly anxious to add to their own stock of knowledge. Some of their first questions, in all probability, will be, —

"Stranger, what mought I call yer name?"

"I mought call it Smith, eh?"

"Well, is trade pooty brisk down your way this summer?"

"What, ye ain't a storekeeper?"

"A doctor then, perhaps?"

"No? Du tell!"

"You've come a pooty considerable ways, I reckon?"

"Morne a hundred miles, have yer?"

"Ye must live somewhar near Boston, then, I calkerlate."

"O, ye live *in* the city, du ye?"

"Know a fellow named Jack Styles?"

"He lives in Boston, I believe."

"Don't?"

"Show!"

And thus our genuine Yankee friend would talk for hours, fully satisfied with our monosyllabic replies.

A near relative to this loquacious individual is the person who always leaves his mark wherever he goes, so that every smooth rock, or beech tree, or guide-post, along the route, proclaims to the wondering public that John Jones, who belongs, perchance, to the I. O. of G. T., or the G. A. R., or some other cabalistic society, has been that way.

But most disagreeable of all is the snobbish tourist, whom we shall occasionally, and, — thank fortune, — only occasionally, meet. It is very seldom that he will deign to notice, much less speak to, such travel-stained, unpretentious pilgrims as we are. But when he does condescend to address us — Well, you know how he will talk; for the snob is the same combination of insipidity, effeminacy, and conceit the world over.

But to return to our party and the Willey House, where we left them meditating on the mutability of human life in general, and the danger of avalanches in particular.

Behind the house stands the hill from which the avalance rolled. Dame Nature, however, has covered with a green mantle of trees and bushes the gashes and chasms which, nearly fifty years ago, were made in its side; and now it looks as peaceful and steadfast as any of the everlasting hills which tower above it. A few rods behind the house we can see the great rock, which so miraculously divided the great, onrushing mass of stones and dirt, and saved the house, while the whole family, who rushed out to save themselves, were destroyed.

Three miles from the Willey House is the far-famed Crawford Hotel; but, our purses not being long, we shall not tarry here a great while, but push on six miles farther, to the White Mountain House, where is not only a good place to encamp, but cheaper accommodation for man and beast than at almost any other hotel in the mountains. This is an important consideration, too, just now, since there are no stores in this region for miles and miles, and we must depend upon some public house for supplies, should the provisions in our wagon give out.

The route thus far travelled has given an abundance of most various and picturesque mountain scenery. There are the perpendicular hills that wall in the Notch, while for some distance we have followed the course of a little babbling, sparkling brook, which, one learns with wonder, expands before long into the broad and impetuous Saco.

Near the Crawford House we notice one guide-board directing to the "Silver Cascade," and another to the "Old Woman of the Mountain." Perhaps the guide-books and boards give this stony matron a more euphonious name than this;

but it takes a stretch of imagination, of which only a mountain hotel-keeper or a guide-book author is capable to see the resemblance which the name indicates, in the jagged piece of rock that is pointed out as the " Old Woman."

But then the Franconia Notch has its " Old Man of the Mountain," and of course the Crawford Notch musn't be without a rival.

It will be very convenient to make the camp at the White Mountain House headquarters for three or four days, and from thence to take excursions to the various points of interest in the neighborhood.

Of course Mount Willard must be climbed — a trip which can easily be accomplished in one day. The view from the summit is more contracted than that from many of its big brothers, to be sure; but, then, it has the advantage of being more distinct, and in the opinion of many no sublimer outlook can be found in all the mountains.

The top of Mount Washington can be easily reached in either of two ways from a camp at the White Mountain House.

In the first place, the ascent can be made by the bridle-path, near the Crawford House, a comparatively easy climb of nine miles; or we can follow the railroad track to the top, a route which shortens the ascent to three miles, though it makes it much more steep and difficult.

If there are any ladies in the party, the bridle-path will be wisely chosen; but no matter which way is taken, the travellers will be tired enough when they reach the top. Not wishing to pay a dollar and a half for the privilege of spending the night at one of the tip-top hotels, and it being impossible to encamp on the summit with any degree of comfort or safety, there is yet a way to accomplish the desired result of being there at sunrise. For a small consideration, and perhaps free gratis, permission may be obtained to spread our blankets on the floor of the depot, where we shall doubtless sleep as soundly as though the mercury was not down to the freezing-point, and the wind blowing fifty miles an hour outside. But let us hope that the sun may rise clear to-morrow morning, for if it does not we shall carry through life, whenever we think of Mount Washington, only the remembrance of a jagged pile of rocks, surmounted by two or three stone barracks, while in all, and through all, and over all, is this cold, wet, drizzly fog, the very thought of which will make one shiver on a dog day. But if it be clear and bright, no words can describe the wondrous scenes that will unfold, and no past fatigue can be weighed in the balance against the satisfaction of the hour.

A visit to Tuckerman's Ravine, and a side excursion to one of the patches of snow, so that we can boast to our friends at home of a game of snow-balling in the middle of summer, will consume a large part of the day, and we probably shall not reach our camp at the White Mountain House before nightfall.

Great as is our wonder at the grandeur of nature upon these mountain tops, it is not unmixed with feelings of admiration for the ingenuity of man in overcoming the difficulties of ascent.

The railroad is a standing marvel. As is well

known, it climbs the mountain in three miles, which necessitates a rise on an average of one foot in four, and sometimes as steep as one foot in three.

The single passenger coach is pushed slowly before the engine, while, so steep is the grade, that the forward end of this little car (not half as long as an ordinary passenger car) is more than ten feet higher than the rear.

Travel on such a road would seem to be accompanied with unnumbered dangers; but so perfect is the system of cogs and brakes that not an accident to life or limb has yet occurred.

The originator and builder of the road says he does not wonder that people ridiculed his idea when he first proposed to run a train of cars to the top of Mount Washington; nor can we wonder either, as we climb carefully down the gaping trestle-work on which the tracks are laid, or struggle over the roots and stones which obstruct the " Fabyan Path ; " poetically so called, we presume, for it is without doubt the worst little trail that ever led down a mountain side.

By devoting three days and a few dollars more to the White Hills, we can go around the mountain, and see the beauties of the glen, the emerald pool, Glen Ellis Falls, &c.; but if the three weeks and fifteen dollars limits proposed at the outset are adhered to, the tent must be struck on the next morning after the visit to the monarch of these hills, and the line of march for the Franconias be taken up.

The first day's journey takes the party by the Twin Mountain House, — one of the finest of the mountain hotels, which during some seasons has been able to offer the unusual attractions of "Beecher every Sunday, and dances every evening," — through the pretty little village of Bethlehem, and just at nightfall, after toiling up three or four miles of a most leg-wearying hill, brings the party into the very heart of the Franconia Mountains, and more than two thousand feet above the sea level.

These hills are so heavily wooded that it is not easy to find a cleared place large enough to pitch the tent, much less to pasture a horse; consequently the beast must be stabled at the Profile House barns, which will cost a dollar a day; and if the little shanty, called the Summit House, about a mile from the Profile Hotel, is empty, it will be best to spread our blankets on the floor, and after making a smudge of chips for the benefit of the mosquitos, consign ourselves to the charge of Morpheus.

Of course, one day must be spent in trouting; it wouldn't do to go to the mountains and not have a fish story to carry home to one's friends. So we shall undoubtedly start off for the brooks, one of these bright mornings, with worms enough to feed a trout pond, and line enough dangling from our poles to supply a mackerel schooner. What exultation we feel as we think of the possibilities of sport and trout, which are before us to-day! There tumbles the little mountain brook, with its deep holes and shady nooks, each one containing a speckled beauty, that we are sure was foreordained to bite our tempting bait this very morning; for why should we not have as good luck as the Mr. A. we read about in the paper, last week, who in one half day caught seventy-nine trout, all weighing over a pound apiece?

Ah! Won't Bill Harris open his eyes when we tell him of that great string we caught,— shall catch, we should say, for we have just dropped our hook over the edge of that mossy log, where it looks so black and deep?

There, we have a bite so soon, but it is on the back of the hand that holds the pole; and as we bring the other hand down upon it with a vindictive slap, we jerk the pole, and the hook is caught fast in the mossy log.

Ten minutes of vexatious work on the slippery rocks and log unfasten the hook, and we drop it in again, just where the water eddies round that big stone. And now we have a *bona fide* trout bite, so quick and sharp (no nibbling and fooling with the bait for a trout), and up we pull in great excitement to see our line firmly caught in a limb six feet over our head, and the trout darting off to another rock to tell his friends of his adventure.

Already we are prepared to pronounce the man who caught those seventy-nine trout a fraud; and by the time we have shinned up the tree and disentangled the line, we can, with a hearty good will, anathematize trout, and lines, and trees, and everything else connected with brook fishing.

We have learned two things, however: first, that three or four feet of line are better than a dozen, when fishing along these wooded streams, and that a quick but quiet jerk is more likely to bring up a fish than a furious one.

If we learn as much as this every time we lose a fish, we shall, no doubt, go back to the summit shanty at night, with the prospect of enjoying a good trout supper, and with the proud consciousness of having a very respectable fish story to relate to Bill Harris when we get home.

If the next morning is pleasant, there is a prospect of one of the most delightful days yet spent among the mountains, for the quiet beauties of the Franconias are all to be seen, and most of them can be easily seen in one day.

One of the most pleasant sensations about these excursions, to one starting off, lively and spirited, in the cool of early morning, is that of entire freedom from the care and worry of ordinary life.

What does it matter whether gold is $111\frac{3}{8}$ or $111\frac{1}{2}$? Cotton may be light and rising, but it cannot be lighter than our spirits; while sugar may be depressed and gunny-bags dull without having any corresponding effect upon our feelings.

Old Granny Brown may have the pip, and need a bread pill, but her complaints can't reach our ears; or, if we chance to belong to the clerical profession, we shall find that we left our Hebrew roots and knotty doctrines at home with our black coats and ministerial neck-ties.

Echo Lake is the first point of interest reached after leaving camp, and it is well worthy of the hour devoted to it. A perfect sparkling gem it is, set in the green and gray of the surrounding mountains, which in some places rise perpendicularly from the water's edge. But as the name indicates, the echo is *the* attraction of the little lake, for the mountains are placed at such an angle that the report of a pistol or a blast from the huge tin horn which the guide carries, is caught and played at shuttlecock, by them, thrown from one to the other, time after time, until at length the poor little noise is entirely worn out, and dies away in the distance.

Half a mile from Echo Lake is the Profile House, and a few rods beyond (forty, we believe, is the exact number) is the best place to view the " Old Man of the Mountains " for whom the hotel was named. The old gentleman is of a very modest, retiring nature, and as he can not very well retreat from the vulgar gaze, he often draws a cloudy veil over his features.

Should he be propitious, however, and show himself, we could sit for hours on the rough little seat which has been erected by the roadside, and gaze on his rocky profile, as the lights and shadows play over it, far up there in cloudland, thinking of Whittier's graphic lines, —

> "Like a sun-rimmed cloud
> The great Notch Mountains shone,
> Watched over by that solemn browed
> And awful face of stone,"—

as well as of many other sublime and poetic things; and endeavoring to get all the glimpses we can of the "Old Man's" face, as we continue our walk towards the Flume.

The next object of interest reached is the "Basin," which is hollowed out of the solid rock as smoothly and regularly as though just from the shop of a city plumber. Though it looks scarcely six feet deep, and the whole bottom can be distinctly seen, the natives (relying doubtless upon the well-known gullibility of tourists) tell wonderful stories in regard to its depth. It is a very moderate guide who falls short of forty feet.

Four or five miles below the Profile House stands the Flume House, and not far from here we take a path which the guide-board tells us leads to "The Pool;" for we are determined to investigate to-day all the natural curiosities that lie in our way.

The Pool is simply an enlarged basin, with more turbid water, and of a less perfect shape. The most curious thing connected with the Pool is the grizzly old philosopher who spends his summers beside it, dispensing maple sugar and lemonade to all visitors. Besides compounding for us a very good pitcher of lemonade, this modern Aristotle (he can hardly be called a peripatetic philosopher, however, for he rows rather than walks about) will invite us to take seats in his boat, and for the moderate consideration of twenty-five cents, he will explain to us his theory of cosmography while he rows us slowly about the Pool.

This cosmography of his is simply a rehash of Captain Symmes's theory of concentric circles, and is based on the singular fancy that the earth is hollow, and inhabited inside, where continents correspond to seas upon the outside, and vice versa. Our interterrestrial cousins are supplied with air and sunlight, according to this philosopher, by means of big holes at either pole; and in his opinion they lead very much the same kind of lives as we poor mortals do upon the outside. Our philosophic boatman supports his romantic notions with various arguments (among which the Caspian Sea, which has no outlet, and the tropical plants which have been found far within the borders of the arctic circle, figure largely), and illustrates them with diagrams of the earth, as he would have it, painted upon a smooth rock, which walls in one side of the Pool.

To those who wish to investigate the mysteries of cosmography still farther, our friend will sell a small pamphlet, which he has written upon this subject, to which he has appended a string of recommendations from the late sovereign of France, the emperor of China, and other potentates, high and mighty, all of which were doubtless sent in a batch by some waggish rogue.

Not more than half a mile distant from the Pool is the Flume, the goal of this day's walk, and decidedly the most remarkable sight yet found among the mountains. The straight, narrow passage, the lofty walls of rock which tower on either side, as though built by some Titanic mason, the rushing, boiling brook beneath our feet, the immense boulder caught between the walls of the Flume directly over our heads, which it seems as though a breath would send crashing down, — all conspire to produce an impression which no other mountain scene has produced.

But the garden of Eden had its serpent; and the Flume, as well as every other place in the mountains, has its pest in the shape of a mosquito or midge. Our ancestors used to believe that the father of lies appeared to them in various shapes, as a goat, or hare, or black cat; had they lived among the White Mountains, they would have embodied him in a mosquito, or midge, or black fly.

It is singular what a small affair will bring you tumbling down from the sublime to the ridiculous. You may be gazing awe-struck upon the wonderful beauties of the Flume; grand and poetic thoughts are coursing through your soul, when, suddenly, a mosquito settles upon the end of your nose, or a midge insinuates himself into the back of your neck; instantly the sublime and beautiful vanish, the bitten member becomes the centre of sensation, and fruitless assaults upon the offending insect take the place of rapt meditation on the beauties of Nature.

This is one of the ills of camp life which can't be cured, and so must be endured with the best grace possible. We kill a hundred of our tormentors, and a thousand will come to the funeral; we smear our hands and faces with kerosene oil, but, while it greatly offends our own senses, the mosquitos seem to *prefer* their blood-puddings flavored with petroleum. We hear all sorts of herbs and unguents recommended, and apply a liberal quantity to our devoted features. The midges are attracted all the more, and revel in the pennyroyal, or catnip, or camphor, as though the odor and flavor were as agreeable as possible. The only thing which these ubiquitous insects seem to dislike is a thick smudge of black smoke; and as this can easily be raised, with the aid of an old milk-pan and some damp chips, we can be tolerably free from these mountain pests at the expense of turning ourselves into well-seasoned hams.

We have now seen the principal points of interest about the Franconia Notch, and, if we take one more day to ascend Mount Lafayette, we can feel that we have "done" the mountains quite thoroughly.

There are many more charming places to visit, to be sure, and many more mountain peaks to scale, among which we might spend several delightful weeks; but already we have seen the points of most note, and a great deal more than many of those who spend ten times as much money on their summer vacation.

Then, if we are all agreed that it is time to start for home, we will roll up our blankets, stow away the small remnant of our provisions in the hard tack barrel, and, with a cheer for the Summit shanty which has so kindly sheltered us for the past few days, we will be off down the mountain.

Should we wish to vary our homeward route, we can turn to the south-west instead of the south-east. In this case, the first camp should be in Landaff, and the second in Haverhill, where we strike the Connecticut River.

Of course, if any of the party are utterly disgusted with " roughing it," they can here take the cars, which, for a few dollars, will land them near their homes. But if the vote is for camp life still, as, no doubt, it will be, it will be found that no part of the trip has been pleasanter than this journey down the valley of the lovely " willow-fringed Connecticut."

Now see what the trip has cost us, and never again say that you cannot afford to go to the mountains.

Horse at one dollar per day for three weeks, ...	$21.00
Wagon, ...	5.00
Hard tack and other provisions, .	22.00

Tent and stove hire, . . .	4.00
Feed for horse on the way, .	12.00
Provisions bought on the way, .	15.00
Plates and cooking utensils, .	3.00
Incidentals, ...	8.00
Total, ...	$90.00

This sum, divided among six individuals, makes each one's share of the expenses fifteen dollars, for a three weeks' excursion to the White Mountains.

CHAPTER III.

TO CANADA. — MONTREAL. — QUEBEC. — OTTAWA. — RIVER ST. LAWRENCE.

IF you were ever a small boy, and if at that time you studied common school geography, you must often have gazed at the variegated sections of pigment which are supposed to indicate to the youthful mind the various countries of Europe, and wished yourself in the very middle of those countries. Do you remember how one yellow patch, standing for England, represented to your juvenile imagination the great Tower of London, and the British Museum, and the Tunnel under the Thames? Do you remember how gay Paris, with its Notre Dame, and Tuileries, and all its other wonders, whose names you couldn't pronounce, peeped out at you from the green section which was bounded by the Alps and the

Pyrenees? and how you always heard the great bell of Moscow and the big guns of the Kremlin thunder out whenever you looked at that large spot of blue paint called Russia? And do you remember how you longed, with all your heart and soul, to see these wonders in reality?

If any boy has not had these thoughts and desires, let us pity his unimaginative little soul, and predict for him that future which people so expressively imply, when they say, "He is a very *good* man, but he will never set the river on fire." To be sure, many men lose their desires for travel when they get out of their teens, and would not exchange their walk through State Street for any Boulevards of Paris; but there are many more who are as eager to visit Europe in manhood as when they first dog-eared their geography in the school-room, but who are kept at home by the thousand leagues of brine which roll between the two continents, and by the insurmountable barrier to bridging over this gulf which a lean pocket-book presents.

To all such Canada invitingly offers itself.

Here are France and England combined in a small way. To be sure, you will not find the Louvre or St. Paul's, and the *patois* will neither be purely Parisian nor thoroughly Cockney; but in many respects you will see very good representatives of the two great old world countries in this new world province. For instance, when you step off the cars at Montreal, you will notice that the streets named St. Jean and St. Pierre, as well as St. John and St. Peter, and that the Rue Josephine and Notre Dame run side by side with Dorchester and Main Streets.

At one store you step into, you will get perfectly distracted with the volley of French sentences which the voluble Celt shoots out at you, while in the next the stout John Bull, in gray clothes and bushy side-whiskers, will inform you, perchance, that the portrait you are looking at is a " 'andsome picture of Prince Harthur, done hin Hindia hink."

It is one of an author's privileges to take it for granted that his readers agree with him in all his assumptions, even if he hasn't attempted to prove them very conclusively; therefore it is assumed, without arguing the point any farther, that Canada is a most desirable place in which to spend a summer vacation, and it only remains to tell how and for what expense the sights of the New Dominion can be seen.

And first we shall want to purchase a round-trip ticket by one of the great railroad lines which connect Canada with the United States.

The price of these tickets varies slightly from year to year, but as a general thing, an excursion ticket can be bought from Boston to Montreal and return for twenty dollars, and to Quebec and return for twenty-two dollars.

Other things being equal, it is better to purchase tickets by way of the Boston and Lowell and the Central Vermont railroads; as by this route we shall be sure of obliging officials, smooth road-beds, and easy-running cars, — advantages which all roads cannot boast, by any means. But of course, in the case of such poverty-stricken persons as we are supposed now to be, a few jolts and jounces more or less do not matter much if many dollars can be saved by enduring them; so we shall go by the line which offers to take us to Montreal the cheapest.

And just here, before stepping aboard the train, a few words in advance in regard to the expense. An interesting letter from Montreal, lately published, closed by saying that "with due economy the trip might be taken for a hundred dollars." Why, my dear sir, with due economy the trip may be taken for half that sum!

But do you say, "Then must we be close, and count every copper, and live in a mean sort of a way generally?" By no means. To be sure, we cannot indulge in a great many game suppers, or eat sandwiches filled with bank bills, a la Lord Timothy Dexter; but the routes of travel are just the same, the rivers just as broad, the mountains just as grand, and the scenery just as novel to the poor man as to the rich. The hotels we shall stop at may not be nearly as expensive, but they may be guaranteed equal in solid comfort to those which our rich neighbors patronize.

No doubt it would be pleasant to scatter the greenbacks right and left; to buy a black silk for aunt Jane, and a set of jewelry for Mary Ann, and a whole toy-shop for little Joe, — in short, to have no care or anxiety on the financial score; and when " our ship comes in," or " our uncle from India" arrives, we shall doubtless travel in this way; but until the hypothetical uncle or ship actually comes, will it not be better to take a cheap excursion than to have no summer vacation at all?

Again assuming that there is a unanimous vote in agreement with these sentiments, we will step aboard the waiting train in the magnificent new Lowell Railroad station. The clock points to the hour of starting, the conductor shouts, " All aboard!" and off we are.

By the spindle cities of Lowell, Nashua, and Manchester we roll, beside the busy Merrimac, picturesque and lovely still, though it is defiled by so many mill-wheels, and regarded by so many sordid eyes as only so much " water-power."

Through New Hampshire's capital, on and on, we are whirled, through the heart of the Granite State, catching many glimpses of faraway mountains, green valleys, and white villages; and a little after noon we cross the Connecticut, and make our first stop of any length at White River Junction, Vermont. "Half an hour for dinner," and then we again take our seats in the cars for a ride through the green hills of stanch Vermont. The scenery in the neighborhood of Waterbury and Montpelier is particularly striking, and we shall be tempted to stop there instead of proceeding.

By supper time we shall reach St. Albans; and no one knows better how to supply our gastronomic wants than Mr. Dunton, whose gong will call us to his attractive dining-room in the station.

Montreal is less than three hours' ride farther on, most of it over Canadian soil, — and a most flat, uninteresting ride it is. The monotony is broken, however, by the flourishing village of St. John, with its big river and numerous vessels; and soon the green waters of the St. Lawrence heave in sight (as we should say, were this a nautical novel), as well as that masterpiece of bridge-building which spans it.

During the ten dark minutes which are occupied in crossing the Victoria Bridge, there is time to call to mind all the dark-tunnel stories, tragic and comic, which a thorough acquaintance with railroad literature will supply. We are so near our destination, too, that it is time to think of what hotel we shall make our headquarters while in the city; for as the principal choice, in Canadian cities, between first and second class hotels, is in the number of dollars *per diem* we shall be obliged to pay, it will be well to know beforehand how much our bill will be.

St. Lawrence Hall is the highest priced house, and next comes the Ottawa Hotel, pleasantly situated on St. James Street. The price of either of these houses would justify the name "first class," though the accommodations would hardly substantiate the claim; at least, according to "American" notions.

And here we must rise to explain, that Canadians universally denominate their cousins of the States "Americans," as distinguished from natives of the Dominion; as though they themselves lived in Malacca or Van Diemen's Land, or anywhere, indeed, but in America. But to return to the subject of hotels. Almost equal in other respects to those we have mentioned, and with charges about half as great, is another class of public houses, such as the Albion, Montreal, and Recollet; the Albion is as good as any, and guests of this house will probably be dissatisfied neither with the accommodations nor with the price.

Montreal, though a pleasant city, is not one in which we shall care to linger a great while, for the very reason that we shall here find little that is novel and strange to our eyes, accustomed to New England cities. Montreal is simply an undersized Boston. The streets here, to be sure, are not so well paved as in the "Hub," neither are there as many fine residences and business houses, nor are the sidewalks as crowded as in our "modern Athens;" but the same spirit of commerce and business enterprise, which gives life to our own cities, has touched this Canadian metropolis as well; the quaint French element is nearly swallowed up in the bustling, busy Anglo-Saxon, and very creditably might Montreal pass for a half-grown Boston, and St. James Street or Notre Dame for a juvenile Washington Street or Tremont Row. There are just four sights, and only four, as far as we have been able to learn, which are particularly worth visiting, namely: The French Cathedral (Notre Dame), the Jesuit Church, the Gray Nunnery, and Mount Royal, with the ride around it.

The first of these attractions is certainly a majestic building; it is one, too, whose greatness grows upon you the more you look upon its massive towers, and gaze down its long aisles. Always open is this great church (like all the Catholic churches), and always is there a stream of humanity pouring through it, now stopping here to touch the precious (dirty) holy water, now there to bow before some crucifix or image, and again to kneel at some sacred shrine.

"The largest church in America, holding ten thousand people," says our veracious guide-book, speaking of this church, both of which statements we should be very much inclined to doubt, were it allowable for a traveller to doubt his guide-book.

But "No disputing the umpire," as the rule is in base ball; so "No doubting the guide-book" must oftentimes be our rule in travelling, since no higher authority presents itself by way of verification. But it is not the long, dim aisles, nor the burning candles and swinging censers, nor yet the saints in blue and gold, which make one or two hours spent in the great cathedral so attractive; but it is the living stream before alluded to.

Here comes a day laborer in his blue blouse, and brick-dust overalls; close behind him follows a richly-dressed young lady, evidently from the "upper ten" of French society. There sits a pale, faded, weary-looking woman, such a one as we always imagine in a close, attic room, with an interminable pile of plain sewing beside her. Not far from her, perhaps, sits a fat, jolly market woman, with fun and laughter gleaming out of her dark French eyes, though she is counting her beads so devoutly. Here and there a sleek, black-robed priest is gliding silently about, waving his incense, or praying with clasped hands for some departed soul, who was so stout a sinner during his lifetime that he needs an additional paternoster now to free him from purgatory.

Yet all alike, priest and people, saint and sinner, rich and poor, seem to worship with reverence and humility; all cross themselves devoutly at the same spot, and all seem to have come in from some other motive than curiosity, or to see the fashions. On our way out we shall be solicited to go up into one of the great towers of the cathedral which mark its resemblance to its namesake in Paris. The magnificent view of the city which we obtain from the top of the tower is well worth the twenty-five cents, which we are charged for an entrance fee, to say nothing of a sight of the great bell, which is said, and probably with truth, to be the largest in the new world. This monstrous bell weighs thirty thousand pounds, and to be once thrilled by its thunderous bass tones is almost enough of itself to repay a visit to Montreal.

The church of the Jesuits, though smaller and far less imposing outside than Notre Dame, is incomparably more beautiful within.

The walls and ceiling are covered with frescoes representing events in the life of Christ and his apostles; and though we have heard would-be artists complain, in a hypercritical way, that these frescoes were mere daubs. scarce worthy of a glance, yet for me and the great majority of ordinary travellers whom we represent, these "daubs" will appear true works of art, and the church which contains them, with its paintings and frescoes, and brilliant windows, and numerous confessionals, is a wonderful church indeed.

The Gray Nunnery is the next place we will visit, and we must time it so as to reach the convent about noon, for then the sisters will all be assembled in the chapel, and we shall have a better chance to peep into their meek faces, hidden away back in their stiff and spotless hoods, and to see their forms of worship, than at any other time.

Everything about the nunnery is immaculately neat and nice, and in the uniforms of gray we discover many sweet, spiritual faces, which contrast favorably with the coarse features of the priests, many of whom, evidently, do not consider high living and good cheer incompatible with their sacred office. Still, as we leave the convent, a feeling of relief comes over us, as though we had escaped from a chilling prison air; and we are more convinced than ever that one good home fireside, with the love and happiness which cluster around it, is worth more than the sanctity of all the convents and nunneries in the world.

By "the mountain," in Montreal, is meant Mount Royal, a sizable hill behind the city, which, clothed with foliage to its very top, forms a fine background for the city to which it gave a name.

A ride around "the mountain" we shall doubtless desire to take; and then, when we have spent half a day in walking about the streets, admiring the few fine buildings of which Montreal is justly proud, gazing at the beautiful bronze statue of the queen, and becoming acquainted with the John Bull faces which we meet, we shall be ready to step on board one of the fine steamers of the Richelieu Company for Quebec. For those who have not a round trip ticket, the fare will be three dollars and fifty cents, meals and berths seventy-five cents each, extra. The boats run only in the night, and there will naturally be a feeling of disappointment, at first, at the thought of sailing through this one hundred and eighty miles of St. Lawrence scenery under cover of darkness; but a glance at the monotony of the low, wooded shores, which stretch all the way between these two Canadian cities, will reconcile us to the comfortable night which we shall pass in the state-rooms of the "Quebec" or "Montreal."

Early the next morning the whistle will sound our approach to the walled city of America; and going on deck, we find ourselves at the foot of a precipice, on the top of which are perched houses, and walls, and churches, and fortifications, all huddled together, as though the heavens had opened, some fine morning, and dropped a city all ready made upon this barren rock.

As we step off the boat and into the street, empty and silent as yet, it is so early, we feel almost awestruck, and half imagine that this is an enchanted city, sleeping through its century, until some Prince Perfect shall break the spell. Our fancy is not so far from the truth either, for the dull old city might as well be asleep, so little does it improve or change from year to year.

Prince Perfect frequently arrives, however, in the shape of a rich American; and then the whole city is roused from its lethargy, and sets systematically to work to fleece him. And a Colchian fleece they generally find he yields.

In fact, this gouging of Americans has been reduced to a science in Quebec. We go into a store for a pair of gloves. The polite clerk will pocket our two dollars without remorse, while for the very same article he would not think of charging his Canuck customer more than half that price.

The St. Louis Hotel, the only first-rate one in the city, will coolly charge us three dollars and fifty cents a day, and the Canadian who came on the same boat with us it will charge one dollar and fifty cents or two dollars.

For this reason we will not stop at the St. Louis, but patronize Henchy's, a much less pretentious house, which charges only one dollar and fifty cents *per diem*.

A good breakfast will best prepare us for a day of sight-seeing, and before we go out we will ask our landlord what are the principal sights of the city.

"The Citadel, Plains of Abraham, and the Falls of Montmorenci," he will undoubtedly reply.

Next we accost an Irishmen with the same question.

"Can you tell us the most interesting places to visit about the city?"

"Sure, an' I can. It's the Citidil, an' the Plains of Abraham, and Montmorenci, that ye want to say."

To a Frenchman, perhaps, we next address the same interrogation.

"Monsieur would know ze chef places of intereest. Tres bien. He moost visete ze Plains of Abraham, and ze Ceetadel, — ah, ze Ceetadel and ze Falls of Montmorenci."

So we conclude to visit the Citadel, the Heights of Abraham, and Montmorenci Falls, and to ask no more questions, since they seem to afford us no additional scrap of information.

But, after all, these sights, though necessarily most written and spoken about, are not what best repay us for visiting Quebec.

It is the indescribable air of quaintness, antiquity, and foreignness which most attracts us — the solemn stone houses, the steep roofs, and precipitous streets, rising tier upon tier above each other, in a line so nearly perpendicular, that from one sidewalk you can look straight down the chimneys of the houses on the street below you. Then we are interested in the surrounding wall of masonry, which every now and then bounds our street, and which links this only walled city of America to the mediæval towns of another continent; and all these sights conspire to remove us in spirit four thousand miles to the east and four hundred years into the past.

Here, too, the people are different from any we have met before. Unlike Montreal and other cities of the Dominion, the French element largely predominates.

John Smith must here announce himself as "Advocate" on one side of his office door, and "Avocat" on the other.

"Traverse de Chemin" stares at us from the railroad crossings; and we see many old friends in new dresses posted on the fences and walls.

For instance, even if our French is rather rusty, we are not slow in recognizing " Pastilles Bronchales de Brown," or " Remedies Rapide de Radway."

But while we are making all these observations, wise and otherwise, we may as well be on our way to some point of special interest, which in the first place will undoubtedly be " the Citadel."

Numerous hackmen are certain to be in waiting, as we emerge from the hotel, each urging the claims of his particular vehicle upon our notice, in a most persistent and obstreperous manner; but we shall resist their importunity if we are wise, for the short walk which will take us to all the historic points about the city, will be pleasanter than a ride this bright morning, to say nothing of the three dollars and fifty cents which we shall save thereby.

Perhaps we should here say, that the hackmen will try hard to make us believe that there are a dozen places we want to visit in Quebec, and will supply us with printed lists of these places.

But several of these are Catholic churches, which are simply imitations of Montreal cathedrals, on a much smaller and poorer scale. Still there are one or two other battle-fields and historic points, which we shall like to visit before leaving the city.

One card, which an importunate hackman is perhaps still distributing to visitors, pathetically referred to the spot " where Montgomery was laid out."

Whether this designated the place where the brave general was prepared for burial, or was a slang expression to denote the defeat of the Americans, under General Montgomery, in 1776, is a matter of conjecture; yet the former explanation is the more likely, since it is not easy to believe that a joke ever found its way into or out of the head of a Quebec hackman.

The Citadel is only about half a mile from our hotel, in a south-westerly direction. Through a long, winding way we walk, walled in on both sides by high, massive, granite fortifications, while here and there we see tomb-like iron doors opening into the bank, which are the entrances to the bomb-proof magazines.

By and by we come to the arched gate-way of the Citadel; and here, if we ask permission to see the fortress, the red-coated sentry will send another red-coat to show us about the grounds. A half hour spent in wandering over the Citadel will give one a very good idea of "the terrible enginery of war." Everything looks belligerent — the massive walls, built to withstand a thousand bombs, the pyramidal piles of balls and shells, the glistening stacks of arms, and, above all, the great guns. Just now, it is true, they are basking their huge black bodies in the morning sun, peacefully enough; but it is evident that at any moment they are ready to belch out destruction from a hundred grinning mouths upon any hostile vessel which might attempt the passage of the river.

The view from the parapet is superb. On the right is Point Levis, with its fortifications, ready to aid the Citadel in its deadly work. On the left stretch the gently-rounded Beauport Hills;

far away in the blue distance, and nearer at hand as well, the St. Charles comes winding slowly down to meet the St. Lawrence; while directly beneath our feet lies the sleepy old city, which, encircled by its zigzag wall, looks as though it might have remained unaltered since the day when Charlevoix first landed on the banks of the St. Charles, more than two and a half centuries ago.

Our soldier-guide will point out, among the other prison-like structures of the upper town, the old Parliament Buildings and Laval University; and we shall notice the piles of lumber, and innumerable rafts, which give quite an air of life and activity to the lower town.

In former years a very large garrison was stationed at Quebec; but gradually the troops have been withdrawn, until now only one hundred and sixty red-coats guard the Citadel.

A walk of a mile farther beyond the fortress brings us to historic ground, for these level, green cow-pastures, which surround us after we pass the toll-gate, are none other than the far-famed "Plains of Abraham."

On the left hand side of the road is Wolfe's monument, with this grandly simple inscription, in memory of the hero who sleeps beneath: —

HERE DIED

WOLFE

VICTORIOUS

SEPT 13TH 1759

Very strongly does this battle-ground impress us, since man has encroached but little upon nature, and we look upon the same scenes that saw the hostile armies of France and England marshalled against each other a hundred years ago and more.

Here are the same steep, slippery banks of clay which the British army found it so difficult to scale; the same dark forest in the background, stretching off indefinitely towards the west, and the same green pastures that then drank the blood of Celt and Saxon.

Now is made clear the wisdom of not yielding to the blandishments of the hackmen, who wished to "show the sights." What pleasure would there be in visiting these historic heights in the company of a human parrot jabbering away in broken English the story which all learned in their school-days? How could one grow heroic in soul, thinking of the two great commanders who, just here, where we are standing, fought so bravely and died so nobly, when all the time an eternal French tongue is sounding the well-learned story of their praise in one's ears! No! No! Let us have no guides or hackmen about us at such a place.

In the heart of the city stands a granite shaft, inscribed on one side with the name of Montcalm; on the other with that of Wolfe. Thus most appropriately has a single monument been erected to the two hostile generals, whose equal courage, patriotism, and skill deserve the same memorial. The inscription on the monument reads, —

MORTEM. VIRTVS. COMMVNEM.
FAMAM. HISTORIA.
MONVMENTVM. POSTERITAS.
DEDIT.*

To vary our route back to the city, we can cut across the fields to the St. Foy road, which runs parallel with the St. Louis, by which we came out.

About a mile from the city, on the St. Foy road, is an iron pillar, surmounted by a bronze statue, raised to commemorate the resting-place of a number of French soldiers, whose bones, a few years ago, were collected and placed beneath this monument.

Now we have seen two of the lions of Quebec; but the Falls of Montmorenci remain to be visited, before we can conscientiously say, "Veni, vidi." These famous falls are eight miles from the city; and the best way of getting there is by chartering one of the strange-looking vehicles

* Their valor caused their death; History gave them equal renown; Posterity a monument.

called calashes. The driver will charge us a dollar and a half for the ride to the falls, if we make a bargain with him in advance, and the novel sensation of a calash-ride will be fully worth the money, to say nothing of the waterfall for which we are bound.

To vary a well-known apothegm, " Show me the carriages of a people, and I will tell you of their civilization." The calash, used nowhere in America except in Quebec, shows plainly that the old city has dropped behind the rest of the world a hundred years, and still belongs to the eighteenth century. This antiquated vehicle has two wheels, which make up in size for any lack in number, and two seats, one narrow one for the driver in front, and another one behind, broader, and very high, for the passengers.

With a hop, skip, and jump we manage to reach our elevated perch behind the driver. The person who has never been in one before, at first holds on to the sides for dear life, imagining that he is riding on a camel's hump, or up in a balloon, or anywhere, indeed, but in a sober, old-fashioned carriage, much more antiquated than the deacon's one-horse shay. But after being bounced and jolted safely through a hundred mud-holes, with which the wretched streets of Quebec are filled, he begins to gain confidence, and quite to enjoy his elevated position. The raw-boned nag shows his best paces under a vigorous application of the driver's whip, and we bounce out of the city, and over the substantial bridge which spans the St. Charles, in quite a lively manner.

The country all along the route seems very fertile and well cultivated, while the scenery is magnificent. On one side rise the lovely hills of Beauport, on the other rolls the broad, irresistible current of the great river. Occasionally the French driver, if we are so unfortunate as to have one, ventures an unintelligible remark of explanation, and we return a grunt that is meant to be appreciative; but, on the whole, efforts at conversation with him are failures, and we soon relapse into complete silence.

This is not wholly a misfortune, however; for there is plenty to interest and amuse by the roadside — the queer little stone cottages, with steep roofs turned up near the eaves; the gaudy little churches, evidently the objects of much respect and veneration; the crosses and crucifixes by the roadside; the women in the fields working out a practical solution of the woman's rights question, while their husbands, loafing quietly at home, sit on their doorsteps, engaged in the arduous duty of smoking dirty clay pipes.

Indeed, the women here seem to do all the work, from tending the baby to ploughing the cornfield; and of the hundred field laborers whom we shall see between Quebec and Montmorenci, probably nine tenths of them will be brawny Amazons.

Another thing which will strike the stranger as singular will be the great number of beggars of all ages and descriptions. The aptitude of the Latin races for begging is wonderful. With them anything which will excite the sympathy of a stranger is invaluable.

A club foot or hunch back is a fortune in itself, while a wooden leg or a blind eye is just so much stock in trade.

From a dozen houses along the road, little girls will emerge with a glass of water in one hand and a worthless bouquet of dandelions and whiteweed in the other, hoping that we shall drink the water, and then feel obliged to buy the bouquet with a ninepence or a shilling. Little boys will run before the calash for rods, holding out chubby hands in a beseeching manner, while stout men will sit in their doorways, and present their hats, as we ride by, with the most perfect " sick-wife-and-seven-fatherless-children " expression on their faces that was ever invented.

After about an hour's ride, our calash will draw up in front of one of the French cottages, and after registering our names within, a small boy will be sent to show us the falls.

Not that a small boy is at all necessary; on the other hand, he is a decided nuisance, since he speaks nothing but French, and our attempts to find out the height of the falls, or the length of the river, or any other little item, is a most aggravating failure; but, then, we are expected to give our mite of a guide a silver bit when we leave him, and this imposition is of a piece with a dozen other extortions which will be practised.

For, say what you will about Yankee shrewdness and greed of gain, Brother Jonathan is far outdone, in this respect, by his cousin across the line.

For instance, though we pay our driver a good price for our ride, he obliges us to pay all the tolls over the bridges and turnpikes; then, when we reach the falls, a quarter of a dollar is demanded before we can enter the narrow gate which is the only entrance to the cataract; neither is our Jehu satisfied yet with the fleece he has plucked, but, when he has at length landed us safely in Quebec, and we come to settle for our calash, he demands, with a piteous whine, that we "remember the driver," which we assure him we will do to our dying day, and never hire him again, should we come to Quebec a thousand times.

However, when we actually catch a glimpse

of the charming Montmorenci Fall, our annoyances will disappear with the mist which rises from the cataract's foot.

A leap of two hundred and fifty feet sheer down does the Montmorenci take over the ledge of friable stone, unbroken by a single projecting rock, while at the base of the ledge the little river is entirely broken up and lost in a seething caldron of foam and spray, and rainbow colored mist, part of which rises up again two hundred and fifty feet, to the bank above, seeking the spot from which it fell.

Soon, however, the river recovers from its fall, collects its scattered forces, and flows on quietly enough to the broad St. Lawrence, which waits for it only a few rods below.

Having seen the falls, we are ready to bid good by to Quebec, unless we care to spend another day in the cathedrals and convents, viewing the relics of departed saints, and the worship paid them by living sinners.

We shall be strongly tempted now, unless our purse is already much exhausted, to turn our faces northward and Saguenay-ward. A visit to the Saguenay would add about fifteen dollars to our expenses; but the trip need not be described, since much has recently been written upon it, and since the present plan is to visit another section of the Dominion.

And now, the excursion to Montreal and Quebec being finished, and as we do not mean to "go it blind" in regard to our financial condition, let us reckon up what this vacation in Canada has cost. Here are the items: —

Ticket to Montreal, Quebec, and return, $22.00
Hotel bill at Montreal, for four days, . . 8.00
" " Quebec, for three days, . . 4.50
Incidental expenses, including carriage hire, meals, and berths on cars, and boats, &c., &c., discount, &c., ... 15.00

Making our total expenses for a trip of ten days, in Canada, ... $49.50

For about the same expense can one spend

another vacation in the new Dominion, turning westward, instead of eastward, from Montreal. Though this route has not yet become so popular with pleasure-seekers as the one just described, perhaps it possesses even greater attractions for many, since it shows more of the wonderful river scenery of Canada, and the newer and more enterprising sections of the Dominion.

This excursion, moreover, will introduce us to the Canadian capital, and to the greatest lumber region of the world, as well as to the exciting sport of running the rapids of the St. Lawrence, on our way back to Montreal.

Early in the morning, if we decide in favor of the Ottawa trip, we shall take the cars at the Grand Trunk station, on Bonaventure Street, Montreal; and seven miles from the city, the cars will transfer their freight to the trim little steamer, which is here waiting to take us half way to Ottawa. Soon we shall be ploughing our way through the turbid waters of the Ottawa, which look about the color of muddy cider.

If we were not in a country of great rivers, the Ottawa itself would be a standing marvel, for there are very few rivers in the world that outrank it in size.

Noted for its great volume and the impetuosity of its course, it sweeps down for hundreds and hundreds of miles from its undiscovered source in the far north. For more than a thousand miles from its union with the St. Lawrence have explorers traced its course, and yet its head waters have never been reached, and it is not certainly known whether the Indian tradition that it rises in a great lake, as large as Lake Huron, is true or false.

No wonder that in the Indian tongue this mighty stream is called the Kitchesippi, or great river.

Soon after taking the steamer, we reach the old French town of St. Anne's, with its big church and little houses; and, to avoid a rapid, we here have to pass through a lock, during which rather slow operation, we have a good chance to see this old-fashioned village, and a large proportion of its inhabitants, who make an unfailing pilgrimage to the wharf to see the great event of the day — the arrival of the boat.

Here at St. Anne's it is said that the poet Moore wrote his immortal Canadian Boat Song, the chorus of which —

> " Row, brothers, row; the stream runs fast;
> The rapids are near and the daylight's past " —

is so familiar to all. Surely the lovely scene of river and rapids, green islands and fields, and gently-sloping hills, which the poet looked out upon from St. Anne's, was enough to inspire a more prosaic soul than Tom Moore's.

One of the most noticeable features of our ride up the Ottawa is the immense amount of lumber floating down the river, both in rafts of rough logs and barges piled with boards. Perhaps a short account of this greatest industry of Northern Canada will not be uninteresting.

The first step of the lumberman is to secure of the government, which owns most of the timber-land of Canada, a berth, or limit of woodland, on the Upper Ottawa, or on one of its tributaries.

These limits are sold by auction for a merely nominal price, something like a dollar or a dollar and a half per square mile.

A limit, which usually comprises about a hundred square miles, having been secured, Indian scouts are sent out to find and mark the position of the best pine grove in the tract.

When the cold weather actually sets in, an army of five or six hundred lumbermen is despatched to this limit, and then from October to April the woods are merry enough with the cheery ring of the axe, and the shout of the many teamsters.

On first reaching the limit, a rough shanty of logs is built, with a double row of berths around the sides, a raised fireplace in the centre, and an opening in the roof which serves as a chimney. And this rough hovel gives a name to everything connected with lumbering. For instance, "shantying," in common parlance, means lumbering; "going up to shanty" is going to the lumber camp. Lumbermen, in this "shanty dialect," are "shanty men," and the horses they take with them are "shanty horses."

The domestic economy of the shanty is conducted on very simple, and, withal, strictly temperance principles.

The staple articles of diet are fat salt pork and doughnuts, while tea is the universal beverage. But such tea! — it does not even bear a family resemblance to the delicious drink of a well-ordered supper table. Such tea would be no more appreciated by the rough palate of a "shanty man," than would a Parker House dinner by a Mississippi alligator.

Would you know the recipe for shanty tea?

In a pot of cold water place two heaping handfuls of tea, hang it on the crane over the fire, and let it boil — not simmer, but actually boil — for half an hour; then sweeten with molasses, and you have the favorite drink of the Canadian lumbermen.

Some of the supplies which are required by a gang of six hundred men throughout the winter are as follows: —

825 barrels of pork,
900 barrels of flour,
7,500 pounds of tea,
3,650 gallons of sirup,
6,000 pounds of tobacco,
375 dogs,
225 sleds, &c.; &c.,

the whole, costing over fifty thousand dollars, at a low estimate.

When spring comes, the logs are hauled to the nearest stream, and then floated down, through various tributaries, perhaps, until at length they reach the broad Ottawa.

When the rafts reach the Chaudière, near Ottawa City, they are caught by a boom; and in the immense steam saw-mills which here line the river, they are speedily converted into the building-material of the world.

Now that we know something of the history of the rafts and lumber scows which dot the river on every side, let us pay attention to the scenery through which we are passing. Nothing very striking or grand shall we see; but still the quiet beauty of the scene, which is ever unfolding to us, will make this day, spent on the forward deck of the Ottawa steamer, a red-letter day in our Canadian journey.

On the right are the green fields and log huts of the Province of Quebec, and on the left the log huts and green fields of the Province of Ontario, with little of the wonderful difference in the opposite banks observable which many travellers imagine they see in favor of Protestant Ontario, and to the disadvantage of Catholic Quebec.

A single glance at either shore, however, would convince us that we were not passing through any part of Yankee land, such an air of shiftlessness and general debility is everywhere noticeable.

We have been told, too, that the superstitious ignorance of dwellers in these backwood settlements is perfectly marvellous, for this boasted nineteenth century of enlightenment. Not long ago an approaching comet and the predictions of an ignorant priest threw most of the inhabitants of a large Canadian village into consternation, and fully impressed the whole community with the belief that the day of judgment was appointed for exactly five minutes past ten of a bright May morning.

It was less than two years ago that in another priest-ridden village of the Province of Quebec, a nun, of a prophetic turn of mind, announced that there would soon be three days of total darkness, when not only the sun and moon would be darkened, and the stars would refuse to give their light, but even lamps and fires could not be prevailed upon to burn, and only wax candles which had been blessed by the priest would give light.

In consequence of this startling prophecy the merchants of the place drove a flourishing trade in wax candles, the priests filled their pockets with consecration money, and all waited in dread expectancy for the dark days. The appointed days came; but the sun and moon, lamps and fires, all shone as brightly as ever. The reputation of the prophetic nun was fast sinking below par, when, by a fortunate chance, a tremendous thunder shower arose one night.

Forthwith all good Catholics arose and lighted their consecrated tapers; and — *mirabile dictu* — in the course of an hour or two the storm abated, and soon entirely ceased.

Moreover, one devout sister, more zealous than the rest, besides lighting her candle, sprinkled her furniture and carpets with a liberal supply of what she supposed was holy water; but imagine her horror, and the state of her furniture, when she found the next morning, that she had made a mistake, and in her trepidation of the previous night, had used the bottle of hair oil instead of the flask of holy water.

Nevertheless, the prophetic character of the holy nun was established beyond a doubt, though her prediction had not been quite carried out in all its details; and all pious Catholics blessed their stars, and crossed themselves an extra time, when they thought of the great deliverance which their holy candles had wrought out for them.

But we were steaming up the Ottawa River — were we not? About half way between Montreal and Ottawa the Long Sault Rapids will obstruct our further progress by steamer, and we shall be obliged to take to the rails for a few miles. Grenville and Carillon are the termini, and only two stations of the road, and the single car which this railroad boasts might, to all appearances, have served George Stevenson on his first trial trip. An ancient conductor, in a battered beaver hat, of at least seventy summers, (these figures, by the way, will apply, with great truth, either to the conductor or his hat), punches our tickets; a venerable brakeman turns the crank, while the engine puffs and wheezes as though it, too, were afflicted with old age and decrepitude. But it bears us safely around the rapids, and according to the principle of the old proverb, we should not speak ill of such a train. It is possible, too, that in its onward march improvement has by this time reached even the Grenville and Carillon Railroad. In justice it should be said that, in spite of their unprofessional appearance, the officials of this little road afford a most pleasing contrast, in point of politeness and kindness, to many of the conductors and brakemen of larger roads that might be mentioned.

At Carillon another steamer is in waiting, new, and finely furnished, and comparatively large; in short, worthy of her name, in every particular, is the " Peerless."

By more green fields and log huts we steam, with the sombre pine forests stretching away for hundreds of miles in the distance, until at length, just twelve hours after leaving the wharf at Montreal, we glide under the lee of the high, rocky bluff on which the Canadian capital is built.

As usual, the first inquiry upon reaching a new city will be for a hotel. As usual too, in Canadian cities the highest priced, which in Ottawa happens to be the Russell House, is far from first-class, and but little superior to the more moderate houses. At either the Albion or the Daniels the charges are not more than two dollars per day *for Americans*.

One of the strangest freaks of modern legislators, in the opinion of many, was the establishment of the capital of British America at "half-barbarous Ottawa," as a recent writer calls this bright little city.

But when we have taken a stroll over the city, it will not seem such a very bad place for a capital, after all; and we shall be apt to think as favorably of the judgment of those who selected this site as of the man who has presumed to call this pretty city "half-barbarous Ottawa." Handsome blocks of brick and brown stone line the principals streets, and tasteful private residences give anything but an uncivilized aspect to the outskirts of the city.

Northern belles, with sparkling eyes and rosy cheeks, promenade the streets, in company with the nobbiest of young men who sport Malacca canes and blonde side-whiskers in the most approved Canuck style; while many government officials are galloping to and from the Parliament buildings, with a condescending air and rigidity of back-bone that no one but an

Englishman who is conscious of cutting a swell can assume.

Even we shall probably be obliged to confess to a feeling a little too near admiration to be in strict accordance with our republican principles and training, when we are informed by the awe-stricken voice of a native, as we very likely shall be, that his lordship, the governor general, is passing on horseback.

A little story will illustrate the curious gyrations which the wheel of fortune sometimes makes, and at the same time explain why this main street of Ottawa, up and down which we have been pacing, is called Sparks Street. It has been expanded into a very pretty tale in an old number of one of our popular magazines, but as it is hardly supposable that everybody has complete files of Harper, we will give here an outline of the story.

Some fourscore years ago an adventurous and sharp-sighted Yankee, named Wright, wandered up into this part of the world, which was then an untrodden wilderness for near a hundred miles on every side. When this keen, speculative son of the Puritans saw the rich lands just across the river from where Ottawa now stands, he saw at the same time (in his mind's eye) a thriving village on this very spot, of which a happy old man by the name of Wright was the founder as well as Grand Mogul. In short, here, on the banks of the river, he decided to raise his Ebenezer, as the hymn has it, or, in plain Canuck, to build a shanty. And this shanty, with numerous other shanties which soon grouped themselves about it, he called Hull, after the dull little sea-coast village, so familiar to Bostonians, from which he had emigrated.

Now, Mr. Wright waxed great and increased in goods, as he deserved to do, and had many lusty Irishmen to work for him. Among others was one who bore the suggestive patronymic Sparks. Nevertheless, Mr. Sparks's character was in no wise suggested by his name, whether that name brings to mind the love-lorn Benedict, or merely gives a general impression of brightness and instability. On the other hand, Mr.

Sparks was a model of steadiness and good sense, knowing when he had made a good bargain, and very sure that he was on the losing side, when, at the end of the year, Mr. Wright told him that he couldn't pay him for his year's work in money, but that he must take his pay out in land across the river.

No, there was no help for it; money was tighter in Hull or Wrightsville than it is on Wall Street in a panic, and Mr. Wright was obliged to suspend specie payment entirely, and friend Sparks had his choice of taking any number of acres across the river for his pay, or nothing at all. At first he did flare up, to be sure, — as what spark would not? — when blown upon by such a gale of ill-luck, and he called St. Patrick to witness that those acres across the river were not worth a picayune, or a continental, or whatever happened to be the popular expression for worthlessness in the year 18—; and moreover he went on to remark that it was a crying sin to pay a man in such valueless commodity as Canadian wilderness, and that the more a man had of it, the worse off he was, etc. But he was a good, sensible man at bottom, and concluded, as Mr. Wright showed no signs of " resuming," to take a pair of oxen for his season's work, with about two hundred acres across the river, thrown in as a clincher. The years rolled on, and fortune's whirligig revolved as well; Wrightstown, however, followed the example of neither time nor fortune, but came to a complete stand-still. On the other hand, the rocky pastures on the other side of the river began to show signs of life; first one shanty went up, then another; then some soldiers' barracks were reared, and a frame house soon followed them. By and by it began to be whispered that the government had decided to establish there an important military post, and that a great canal was to be dug right through Sparks's worthless wilderness. After all, Sparks began to think " that wasn't such a bad year's work," and, as the money flowed in upon him faster and faster every year, he became more and more assured of the truth of this conviction.

But you know, or can guess, the rest — how Ottawa grew, and how friend Sparks grew with it; how he developed from Sparks the day-laborer into the Hon. Mr. Sparks the millionaire; and you can doubtless imagine a rotund, hearty old man pacing up and down the handsome, busy street to which he had given his name, and recalling that year, long ago, when he worked for Mr. Wright and received a pair of oxen and — well, a little matter of land "across the river."

And how about Mr. Wright and his village?

Very little indeed, for there is Hull to this day about as dead and dull as its namesake of Massachusetts Bay.

But as to the modern city — Ottawa. It might be emphatically called the Lumber City of America. Indeed, the lumber trade is the great and only distinguishing business of this whole region.

From the high bluff on which the city is built, you look down upon hundreds of acres piled fifteen and twenty feet high with sawn lumber, while the immense mills which here line the river, busy night and day, are ever humming their song of industry and wealth.

It is said that, almost without exception, these great establishments are owned by " American" capital and managed by Yankee skill.

When we visit the lower part of the city to inspect the mills and lumber-yards, we shall at the same time admire the wonderful falls of the Chaudière.

Very few rivals and scarce any superiors have these falls in the country.

Though the descent is not great, the vast volume of roaring, boiling water which tumbles over the rough ledge makes the Chaudière no ordinary waterfall.

In the upper part of the city is situated *the* great attraction of Ottawa — the Parliament buildings.

These are really very fine, " the most magnificent on the face of the earth," any Canadian within a radius of forty miles will tell you; and though we may be disposed to take his statement *cum grano salis*, we can readily excuse his pride in his capitol.

The buildings enclose three sides of a quadrangle, and are built principally of a rough brown stone found in that region, and deeply trimmed with Ohio sandstone.

The architecture is Gothic modified to suit the cold Canadian climate, and the buildings have all a wonderful air of taste and symmetry about them, whether viewed near at hand or at a distance; for the clear-cut outlines of the many turrets and the glittering of the numberless gilded spires can be seen miles away, in that pure atmosphere.

The inside, too, well corresponds with the fair exterior, and anything finer than the halls and corridors, legislative apartments, and general offices of the Canadian capitol is seldom to be seen. The main central building contains the chambers of the Senate and House of Commons. They are tastefully and richly upholstered and furnished; the corridors are hung with paintings of the past governor-generals and distinguished men of the provinces; while the sandstone pillars which support the building are richly sculptured with representations of the animal and vegetable productions of the Dominion.

Of the buildings on the sides of the quadrangle, one is taken up with the general offices of government, while the other is devoted in part to the Patent Office, where we can pass two or three very pleasant hours among the various children of the inventors' brain; some valuable, others worthless, some accepted and patented, others rejected. How much care, and toil, and patience, how many trembling hopes and satisfied desires, and ruined plans for wealth and honor, are hidden away in the cases and on the tables of a Patent Office!

Now, what else is there to see? The guide-book, hotel-keeper, and " we " your self-appointed mentor, all answer, "Nothing." On our homeward journey, let us, with your permission, take the most delightful and exciting steamboat ride which the country affords — the trip down the river, through the rapids of the St. Lawrence; that is, if we can pierce the Bœotian intellects of the Ottawa Railway officials, sufficiently to find when the train for Prescott leaves.

The fare to Prescott, the southern terminus of the St. Lawrence and Ottawa Railroad, is two dollars, and the fifty-four miles of this road run through one of the most desolate, barren, stumpy, swampy, in short (for an ordinary stock of adjectives is exhausted in attempting to describe it), utterly forsaken regions on the face of the globe. The scenery is a continuous succession of swampy lowlands and burnt forests, where the dead trees rear their bare, gaunt limbs to heaven in a ghostly, dreary way. The fact is, the country between Prescott and Ottawa, in the matter of dead forest trunks, might easily "stump" the world.

We shall not have a great while to wait at Prescott, if the steamer is on time; and not long after swinging clear of the wharf, we reach the Long Sault Rapids of the St. Lawrence, which continue for nine miles.

But we mustn't be disappointed because this

little ripple and eddy which we see is the Long Sault of which we have heard and dreamed so much. We shall come to the rapids in good earnest pretty soon.

There, do you see that seething, boiling, rushing, white-capped mass of angry waves, just ahead of us? That begins to meet your anticipations — does it not?

Now we are in the midst of the turbulent waters. How the steamer rocks and careens! Now down, down, down in a watery valley, now up on a billowy hill. How she shakes, and shivers, and groans, as though hit by a cannon ball, when she broaches to ever so little, and a billow taps her broadside ever so gently!

Don't let her broach to much more, pilot, or one of these sledge-hammer waves will shiver her to splinters in a twinkling. Though, in fact, accidents rarely occur, this shooting the rapids is not without real excitement and danger.

This we can read in the captain's anxious face as he nervously paces the upper deck just under the wheel-house. Then we must have four experienced pilots at the wheel, and four more at the tiller; eight pairs of sharp eyes on the foaming rapids, and the narrow channel through them; eight pairs of muscular arms directing the rudders. These show the skill and force it requires to run the St. Lawrence Rapids. And here we are gliding out into still water. Were you afraid? O, no! You scorn the imputation. But then you are rather glad the Long Sault is safely passed.

The scenery on either bank is very pleasing; the shores are hard and well defined, not swampy and reedy, as the banks of the Ottawa; the settlements, too, on both sides of us, look more prosperous than those farther north.

Cornwall is a busy, thriving place, on the Canadian shore; and just below lies the old Indian village of St. Regis, with its old-fashioned church and its historic bell.

Many a romantic tale could the tongue of this old bell ring out if it were so disposed. In the first place, it was made in France, and bought by the St. Regis Indians, who were converts to

Christianity, for their new church. While on its way to its new home, on the banks of the St. Lawrence, it was captured by an American privateer, and taken to Salem.

Soon after, it was bought and hung in the old Orthodox Church of Deerfield. What a different call you rung out then, old bell, when you summoned the good deacons and sturdy Puritans of Deerfield to Sabbath worship, from what was expected of you when you were cast in sunny France!

But this bell was never destined for an Orthodox meeting-house; for soon the Indians, hearing of its Protestant occupation, formed an expedition for its recovery, which resulted in the horrible Deerfield butchery, and the recapture of the bell, which they bore back in triumph to St. Regis.

Eleven more rapids (great and small) we shall run before reaching Montreal.

But at length, near evening, we steam up to the busy quays of the Mount Royal city. Our circle of Canadian travel is completed, and our forty-five dollars are nearly gone, as well.

Which do you prefer, gentlemen, Montreal and Quebec, or Montreal, Ottawa, and the St. Lawrence Rapids?

"You pays your money, and you takes your choice."

CHAPTER IV.

THE TENT ON THE BEACH.

Now, reader, since you have climbed the rocky steeps of the White Hills with us, and wandered through the cities and up and down the rivers of the New Dominion in our company, we begin to feel quite familiar with you; and so we make bold to say, " Come to the sea-shore, and spend a week in our tent on the beach."

We do not expect to tell anything that is new about tent life to you, whose canvas has often whitened Cape Cod's sands or Cape Ann's rocks; but this chapter is for the thousands who yearly swelter through the dog days between the brick walls of a city, or in some blistering inland village, utterly unconscious that the cool breezes of the sea and the delights of camp life may be enjoyed for the same five-dollar bill which perchance only half purchases for them the privilege of existing at home, where the mercury ranges among the nineties.

Even for those who think they have not brawn enough to make mountaineers, or a sufficient supply of the "needful" to take the journey to Canada, this method of spending the vacation is perfectly feasible, and they will find it fully as enjoyable as either of the others.

Then, ho for the sea-shore!

Our outfit for the beach will be very similar to the one we had in the mountains, barring of course our horse and wagon.

The chief modifications are, that we shall not need to take so large a supply of ham and hard tack, since, if we are skilful anglers, our hooks will furnish us plenty of fresh fish, and we can doubtless rely on some passing baker's cart, or upon the neighboring country store, to supply us with the staff of life.

In other respects, as regards our tent, hardware and tinware, stove, and minor provisions, we cannot do better, perhaps, than to follow our old plan in the mountain campaign.

Now, where shall we go? is the next question.

Not that there is any lack of camping-grounds; on the other hand, the difficulty lies in choosing between the many equally attractive spots with which our New England coast abounds.

Thus Nantasket, Cohasset, and Chelsea offer their quiet attractions to the lovers of hard, sandy beaches and surf-bathing. Then Nahant, with its long neck of sand, its cliffs and sterile, rocky promontories, presents varied delights to the pleasure-seeker.

If we desire to get farther out of the busy harbor, and more into the arms of old Ocean himself, we can find few pleasanter places to spread our canvas than the region about Gloucester; and the whole coast of Maine affords excellent tenting-grounds if our place of residence or our inclinations lead us to the Pine Tree State.

The great drawback to the places first mentioned is, that they are fast becoming too common resorts for pleasure-seekers, so that nature is almost lost in the crowd of fashionables who yearly throng the sands of Nantasket and the headlands of Nahant, and, what with gardens, and fountains, and elegant residences, the places begin to resemble artificial parks. On the whole, then, let us vote for some spot in the neighborhood of Gloucester as combining the three requisites of camp life — good fishing, good bathing, and good scenery.

But, of course, wherever our party votes to go, we will loyally follow, whether it is to Cape Cod or Cape Ann, Massachusetts Bay or Passamaquoddy. We simply mention Gloucester as a definite place for the benefit of the anxious and aimless who want a summer vacation, and yet know not where to pitch their tent.

Now, if we have by this time reached our camping-ground, up goes our tent in a trice, with the opening to the sea, that we may get the benefit of the afternoon breeze and the glorious view of old Ocean.

We should, if possible, too, choose an airy spot, at some distance from a grove of trees, for there we may hope to be free from that pest of camp life, the mosquito.

While we are making everything tight and tidy inside and out, a committee of two should be detailed to dig a trench, eight or ten inches deep, around the tent, to prevent our being drowned out, should a rainy day or a sharp thunder-shower visit us.

A sleeping-place for the night is now provided, and a certain aching void beneath our belts asserts its right to be considered next; so we all seize our poles and rush for the rocks, with a realizing sense of working for our suppers that we have never before experienced.

Fishing-poles and lines we can doubtless secure from any one of the many little public houses along the shore at a moderate rental, and at the same place we can get a basket of clams, which will serve us for bait this afternoon.

When we have learned the way of cunners, which in the sinful trick of taking the bait without getting caught are past finding out, we shall discard clams for bait, and use sea worms, which we can find in great quantities by digging in the sand at low tide.

Now put a small piece of bait on your hook (if you use half a clam, as you will be sure to do if a greenhorn at cunner-fishing, you will never catch a supper), and drop in just there, where the water looks deep and dark, and now — "the one who catches the first fish is the best fellow."

Neither Izaak Walton nor any of his disciples ever really explained the delight there is in the "gentle craft" to the genuine angler, who is a fisherman by nature.

It is not what he catches, or what he actually knows that he will catch, that makes him sit so patiently all day long on the hard side of the rock, but it is the vast possibilities which are before him.

He never yet caught a whale, to be sure; but who knows that the very next bite may not be from some monster of the deep!

Thus, as we now sit, waiting for our supper to bite before we bite our supper, we may be quite certain, theoretically, that nothing but cunners and sculpins will visit our hooks, with an occasional rock cod or tautog perhaps; but there is the great ocean before us, looking so deep and mysterious, and filled with all manner of swimming things; and is it not possible that some of the more uncommon will conclude to dine off the cold clam which hangs from our hooks?

In short, fishing is a harmless lottery to the man with a large bump of hope and imagination, and though he often draws blanks or insignificant prizes, yet the opera-houses and railroad shares are still in the sea, and perhaps the very next cast of his line will bring one of them up.

Nipper-fishing is no mean sport, however much it may be decried by professionals, for, though nippers are very abundant along all our New England coast, it requires little less skill to catch them than it does their nobler speckled relatives of the mountain streams; and the old salt by our side, who supplies the city market, and who knows just how to bait and when and how to jerk up the fish, will catch ten nippers to our one.

In the course of an hour, however, we shall probably have caught enough little fish for a moderate meal; and the next question which presents itself will be how to prepare them for the frying-pan.

Here is the *modus operandi* of skinning a nipper, and a most important piece of information we shall find it during our stay at the beach.

Hold the fish firmly in your left hand, and with a sharp knife cut off the back fin from the tail to the head, then do the same with the ventral fins. Cut the skin around the head, pull it off with your thumb and finger, break off the head and — there you have it, as nice and white a morsel of fish as ever delighted the soul of an epicure. Soon, when practice has made us more perfect, we can skin two perch a minute with perfect ease.

Now roll the nippers in corn meal, and lay

them in the spider, in which a piece of salt pork is already sizzling; watch them carefully to see that they do not burn, and in fifteen minutes our dish of cunners, delicate, crisp, and brown, is ready to go with our hard tack and coffee.

We shall doubtless find that there is some natural cook in our party (for the necessity of camp life is the mother of culinary invention), who will often regale us with johnnie-cake and corn-dodgers, and those glorious flapjacks which cap the climax of these out-door meals of ours.

But the crowning glory of our camp life is the evening, when the fried cunners have been disposed of, the dishes washed up, and we arrange ourselves for a social talk before the blazing fire of drift-wood.

Here we are, all lying in a row just within the tent door, with our feet toasting at the crackling fire outside.

Here are Sam, and Tom, and Dick, and Jack, and Hiram, whom you met at the mountains; and these names may stand for doctors of divinity, if you choose, for we have no "Reverends," nor "Honorables," nor even "Misters" out here during these two weeks.

It is getting quite dusk outside, and we can almost see gray night coming down in great sheets over the earth.

Lights of all sizes begin to twinkle about us, from the little star of the twelfth magnitude which glimmers in the cottage of the fisherman, to the bright constellation that shines from the light-house tower. Away in the distance gleams a bright revolving light, which every sixty seconds emerges out of darkness, shines full in our faces for an instant with its Polyphemus eye, then slowly recedes and disappears into darkness again for another minute.

Hoarsely and savagely the waves beat against the rocks, albeit they are singing a gentle lullaby compared with the noise they would make should a storm arise. The tide is coming in now, and a few rods from the shore, where, an hour ago, a ledge of rocks rose high out of the water, only the long backbone of the ledge appears, and it takes but little imagination to call it some terrible sea-serpent, and ourselves and companions trembling Laocoons awaiting his approach. You will notice that the fresh sea breeze has a remarkable vivifying effect upon one's memories of Virgil.

"Pile on the drift-wood, Jack, and let us have a rousing old fire to inspire the stories. Why, each of these sticks and branches in our wood-pile has a tale, if we could only unfold it. Who knows from what far-away land that piece of board drifted? From Brazil, perhaps, or from Norway or Australia. That withered palm-branch and piece of bamboo have had quite a journey surely."

If you could see into the darkness of the tent, you would notice stretched out with the rest of us one or two brown and brawny toilers of the sea, who, attracted by our camp fire, have come up "to hear the news," or to ask "the good word."

We are glad to see them, for capital Munchausens are these fishermen, regular Scheherezades, whose stock of wonderful tales would save their lives more than a thousand and one nights with any story-loving sultan of the Indies.

A few judicious questions asked in a *nonchalant* way will set these sunburnt visitors of ours to reeling off yarns which quite eclipse the stories of Captain Marryat himself. Indeed, on any piscatorial point, whether the discourse touches upon the number of cunners he can skin in a minute, or upon the size of the whale he saw last year, our fisherman is ready with facts and figures astounding enough to make any veracious landsman shudder; and very emphatically do we pronounce all his yarns *fish-stories*.

Occasionally, too, one of us ventures a story, not, to be sure, in any spirit of rivalry with the marine Munchausen, but just by way of variety. Sometimes a conundrum goes around the circle, and is then, of course, given up; and so the time passes, until, before we know it, the evening is gone; the deep, regular breathing of one after another of the party announces his departure for dream-land, and the rest declare that it is time to turn in for the night.

So we fasten the tent flap, dowse the glim by turning the candle end for end in the black bottle which serves as a candlestick, and then coil ourselves cosily in our blankets. A verbatim report of what is said and done during one of these glorious evenings in camp, however enjoyably the time is in reality spent, would be very flat and commonplace reading. The sailor's exploits would be pronounced very poor extravaganza, the stories tame, and the conundrums stupid; and so they would sound; for, in order to appreciate them, you must listen to them with the solemn roll of the sea in your ears, and with the ruddy fire-light dancing and flickering over a circle of brown figures in blue shirts. You should be lying in a tent, too, with a dim candle in the back part of it barely giving light enough to make the dark corners weird and ghostly, peopling them with phantoms, and transforming the stove, and the provision basket hung from the ridge-pole, into gnomes and afrits, and the wraiths of departed suppers which they have cooked or held. You may be sure that Sam, and Tom, and Dick, and their stories, are entirely different affairs under such circumstances from what they are when seen by the aid of prosaic printer's ink alone.

The next morning we must be up, bright and early, to catch our breakfast, for the nippers are particularly eager to take our hooks at this time of day, especially if the tide happens to be pretty well in at the same time.

In their dory, a few rods from the rocks, are our friends, who visited us the preceding evening, busily engaged in examining their lobster-traps.

From some of the traps they pull out eight or ten of the green, ungainly creatures, while some yield only two or three, and others none at all. Then, having emptied their traps, they rebait them with sculpins or other fish offal, and sink them again, to beguile more of their many-legged victims.

But what does that hullabaloo from the point of rocks where Tom is fishing, mean?

We all run to the spot, ready for any excitement, and find that Tom's shouts of triumph arise from his capture of a fine rock-cod, whose blood-red scales glisten in the sun-light as he holds it up to our view. A lucky catch, Tom; for there is a good meal in him alone, and no one need sneeze at a fresh rock-cod for breakfast.

The rock-cod (so called because generally caught near rocky shores) resembles the ordinary cod in shape, but is distinguished by his brighter colors, being the most brilliant of all the fish we shall capture.

The rock-cod, too, is generally smaller than the deep-water variety, and its flesh is considered more delicate.

Of the fish we catch from the rocks, the sea-perch (called by the fishermen, indifferently, "cunners," or "nippers") are by far the most numerous. Indeed, you can hardly drop a line from the rocks at any point along the coast from Labrador to the Gulf without getting a bite from these gamy little fish.

They vary in size from three inches to a foot

in length, though they rarely weigh over a pound, and they vary in color as well. For the most-part they are dark above and light below, with wide bands of bright color.

Sometimes, however, we haul up a fellow who is nearly black throughout; and again a bleached specimen, of a decidedly light orange color, comes to the surface. Whether, in the land of the cunners, the blondes or brunettes are considered more beautiful, we have never discovered. Perhaps tastes differ there as well as in other circles.

Like their relatives, the perch of fresh-water streams, they bite boldly, and are very voracious, so that when our clams are exhausted we can use for bait pieces of their dead brethren, which we have before caught.

Wood, in his Natural History, relates an anecdote of a gentleman who hooked a perch, but unfortunately tore out the eye of the poor creature without catching it. He adjusted the eye on the hook, and replaced it in the water, where it had hardly been a minute before the float was violently drawn under the surface. The angler, of course, struck, and found he had captured a fine perch. This, when landed, was discovered to be the same one which had just been mutilated, and which had actually lost its life by devouring its own eye.

Izaak Walton quaintly observes, in regard to the perch (though he speaks of the fresh-water variety), "If there be twenty or forty in a hole, they may be all caught at one standing, one after another; they being, like the wicked of the world, not afraid, though their friends and companions perish in their sight."

When the water is clear, and not too deep, it is a curious thing to watch a school of cunners playing around your hook.

First a lot of small fry will rush out of the seaweed, and have a regular swimming match with each other to see which will first reach your bait.

There — a little fellow grabs it, and runs off vigorously, three or four feet from his companions, like a greedy chicken. But he is too small to swallow the hook, and only steals a little piece of the bait.

But look now! there comes a good half-pounder, slowly gliding out of his dark corner in the cool sea-weed. How indifferent and careless he looks! scarcely deigning to glance at the bait, or the crowd of youngsters about it, like a young dandy to whom the world is as uninteresting as a squeezed orange, and who considers it undignified to express wonder or surprise at anything. For a moment he keeps himself poised by the gentlest possible motion of his fins, and then turns back into his hole, and you think you have seen the last of him.

But wait a moment longer; he will think better of it. There! out of the sea-weed something rushes like a flash; the baby cunners scatter in every direction; your hook is seized with a determined jerk, and a moment later you have him on the rock beside you, all his dignity and indifference gone; now he is nothing but a poor, gasping cunner, flapping, in a very ungraceful sort of a way, in a basket full of his companions in misery — a sad contrast, my poor fellow, to your lordly movements, a few moments ago, among your small brethren in your own element.

Perhaps there is a moral here for the young swell, whose home is not in the sea-weed, to stick to his own element, and not get out of his depth, like the unfortunate cunner; — but this book is not a sermon to young swells.

Sometimes, instead of the quick, decided bite of the cunner or nipper, from which way of biting the sea-perch derives his latter name, we feel our line slowly and heavily drawn under, and pulling it up with considerable difficulty, we find dangling from the end one of the ugliest specimens of the genus *piscis* that swims the sea. With a head bigger than all the rest of him, split entirely in two by a most unfashionable sized mouth, with great, dull, stony eyes, with blotches of livid colors scattered irregularly over his body, and with ugly spines, nine on each side of his head, like a base ball mustache (to repeat an old joke), the sculpin is certainly a frightful looking fish.

He prowls along the bottom, seeking what crustaceæ he may devour; and if our hook happens to come in his way, he sucks it in without hesitation, since all is grist that comes to his mill.

The sculpin is universally detested by fishermen, since he is worthless for food, difficult to handle, and moreover, drives away other fish from the neighborhood. So we follow the fisherman's usual custom of braining the poor fellow before we throw him back into the water (which is the only method yet discovered to prevent his biting again), and then drop in our hooks once more. Perhaps this time we feel a savage pull, and our line is run out to its full length. We may be pretty sure that this bite is from a pollock; and if we succeed in landing him, we shall find we have caught a handsome fish, with a graceful, slender form, and bright, silvery scales.

The pollock we catch near the shore generally weigh from one to two pounds; those caught in deep water have sometimes been known to weigh thirty pounds. Formerly this fish was considered almost worthless for food, as the flesh is quite soft; but we shall find that they make a very good fry, if eaten as soon as they get through wriggling.

We shall probably, too, make the acquaintance of the flounder in the course of our fishing from the rocks; and a curious figure he cuts as we see him on the bottom, through the clear water, floundering along in his party-colored costume, like a state prison convict, brown on one side and white on the other, with his goggle eyes both on the upper side of his head, peering around for his grub.

The tautog is another fish which we shall sometimes catch, and quite a prize we shall consider him, for fried tautog is justly deemed a delicacy. The tautog generally weighs two pounds or over, and much resembles an enlarged cunner, except that it is darker colored and thicker.

But while we have been discussing the different kinds of fish that visit our hook, others of the party have not been idle; and now, by seven o'clock, with our cunners and rock-cod, we surely have a fair prospect of a breakfast, and Sam suggests that we try our hand at a chowder.

The motion being seconded, and unanimously agreed to, we turn our attention to skinning the cunners, slicing the potatoes, and getting the fire well under way. In our deepest pan we place first, a layer of fish, then a stratum of potatoes, with some chips of salt pork, and a few slices of onion thrown in if we have them; cover these with hard tack; then add other strata of fish, potatoes, and hard tack, until the dish is full. Season each layer with salt and pepper, and add enough water to keep the chowder from burning.

Let the whole stratified compound sizzle on the stove, until the potatoes are soft, and the fish peels off the bones; and then, if aunt Susan should rail at us because we have left out the milk, and Monsieur Blot should look contemptuously over the omission of the inevitable bread crumbs, we can laugh in their faces, and tell them we are very sure that a chowder never *tasted* better.

Besides chowders and fries, our bill of fare may be varied with fresh lobsters, which the fishermen will be glad to sell us for five cents apiece, with crabs and clams of our own capturing, and to any greater extent, that our inclinations and the resources of the neighboring country store will allow.

To the hearty lover of nature nothing can be more enjoyable than these days spent at our seashore camp, the whole coast so swarms with animal life of the lower grades. Every rock we sit on, which is ever touched by the sea waves, is rough with little white cockle-shells, whose owners we shall find snugly coiled up within, if we ever burglariously break into the minute abode.

Every wave that rolls at our feet brings to us some form of ocean life.

Perhaps it is the sun-fish, or jelly-fish, which moves through the water with a most graceful undulating motion, contracting and expanding exactly like an umbrella. Very delicate and edible does the jelly-fish appear at first sight, like the clearest of gelatine; but let him lie on the hot rocks and evaporate in the sunshine until the next high tide, and scarcely a trace of him can be found, since he leaves no skeleton for future archæological societies to wrangle over.

Or perhaps the wave presents to us a five-rayed starfish, or brings along the deserted, bleached, and curiously corrugated shell of a sea-urchin, or a sea-cucumber, which so much resembles his namesake of the garden that we are inclined to throw him at once into our pickle-keg. Perhaps it is only a long, slim, slippery sea-weed that the tide brings up, with some unfortunate bivalve which has taken up his abode in its roots; or possibly, as the wave recedes, a back-action crab will come out of his crevice in the rock to see what is going on in the world. Luckless shell-fish these that come within our range of vision, for the crab robbed of his sea-weed covering will soon be broken up for bait, and Cancer himself will speedily go to pot to be served up at our next meal.

It is not probable that fishing for nippers from the rocks will satisfy the piscatorial desires of such enthusiastic anglers as are we, and without doubt we shall want to devote one day, and perhaps several, to deep-sea fishing for cod, and haddock, and mackerel.

Then we must charter a fishing-smack, and a skipper to navigate the craft and furnish the lines and bait. An hour's sail, with a fair breeze, ought to bring us to the fishing-grounds, which our old Palinurus knows as well as we know our father's door-yard, for fishes are not, as many suppose, scattered uniformly throughout the ocean, but live together in communities, largely, and leave other parts of the sea very thinly inhabited.

So it is the business of the experienced tar who is with us to avoid the desert and to guide us, if possible, to the very Pekin of fishdom. Now, when we have cast anchor, we will bait our stout hooks with a generous piece of clam and sink them as many fathoms deep as our skipper advises. Perhaps we shall have to wait long and patiently for the first bite, and perhaps, on the other hand, the line will hardly straighten itself out before a great jerk will announce that the bait has been favorably received in the regions below. Cod and haddock are both strong and sure biting fish, and one rarely fails to draw them in.

Sometimes each member of a codding party will catch great fish at the rate of one a minute for hours, and a muscle-tiring kind of work it then becomes. Most of the fish we shall catch will probably not run over eight or ten pounds in weight. They grow to a much larger size, however, often weighing fifty or sixty and sometimes a hundred pounds. A most important industry, as we all know, is the cod fishery, not only to our own sea-coast towns, but to the French and Canadian fishermen who frequent the Gulf of St. Lawrence and Newfoundland's banks.

An inexhaustible aquarium, too, has the fisherman to draw from, and he need have no fears that the supply will give out, when he remembers that at every spawning, a single cod deposits over a million eggs. To be sure, very few of these eggs hatch out infant codlings, but for the most part they are destroyed by ravenous fish before even a fin or scale appears.

And well is it that it is so, for it has been estimated that, in a very limited number of years, if every egg were allowed to develop into a full-grown cod, the whole ocean would be so thickly filled with them that navigation would be entirely stopped. But we shall be likely to find the actual state of affairs very different from this sitting with arms resting over the taffrail, waiting for the first unwary fish to bite, and doubtless wishing that Providence had allowed a few more eggs to come to maturity.

The haddock, which is caught quite as often as his cousin the cod, is usually about the same size, and resembles him much in general appearance. Haddock abound all along our coast, in summer far outnumbering the cod, while in winter the order is reversed, and cod are more numerous. The haddock may be distinguished by a black line which extends down each side from the gills to the tail, as well as by a dark spot, about the size of a three-cent piece, on either side of the head. Among Roman Catholic fishermen there is a legend that this is the fish which brought up the tribute-money at the command of our Lord, and that the dark spots under the gills are the marks of Peter's fingers.

Perhaps the monotony of cod and haddock will be broken by the advent on deck of an ugly, spiny-backed, long-tailed scate; and possibly one of the party will be fortunate enough to hook a halibut. If this should happen, all will excitedly gather around the lucky man to witness the struggle.

Even the skipper, to whom cod and haddock fishing is a dull, old story, lays aside his black T. D., and shows something like interest in the matter. How the line rattles over the rail as the great fish makes a dive for the bottom! Now it slackens as he returns, and it is necessary to pull a little on the line, to see if he is exhausted. But he is still too fresh to give up the fight, and off he shoots at a tangent, nearly taking his captor with him. Now to the right, now to the left, and then straight down he rushes; but even a halibut cannot struggle forever, and by and by, completely worn out, the noble fellow is drawn on deck. "A hundred pounder, if he weighs an ounce," says the skipper, sententiously.

We must spend at least one half day, before we break camp, in trolling for bluefish — the most exciting of all kinds of sea-fishing.

As we stand here on the rocks, do you see that commotion out in the water half a mile from the shore? That is caused by a school of bluefish, and some of those savage fellows, who are probably now foraging for their breakfast, and bringing terror and destruction to smaller fish, we must have in our frying-pan this noon. So we jump into the dory and row out to the scene of action.

The tackle for this kind of fishing is rather peculiar; since, instead of using any bait, we simply have a piece of bright metal or jig, as it is called, attached with a hook to a strong line. Let one of the party row the dory alongside of the school at a moderate rate, while the rest of the party throw out jigs, which the motion of the boat is sufficient to keep floating on the surface of the water. But the eager bluefish will not give time for so many words of explanation, before, with a fierce splash, he seizes the glittering metal, and is jerked into the boat.

The next moment the spoon (as the jig is often called) is again floating on the wave, to beguile a fresh victim.

We must be careful, however, when pulling in, to keep the line taut, since, if he has a chance, the bluefish will eschew the spoon, not finding it as digestible a morsel as he anticipated, and will disengage himself from the hook. If there is better sport than trolling for bluefish on a clear, breezy summer's day, pray let the world know what it is!

From its resemblance to the common mackerel, the bluefish is often called the horse-mackerel, though improperly, for the horse-mackerel is quite a different fish. It derives its name "bluefish" from the color of the upper part of its body; and we shall find, at dinner time, that it is just as capital a fish to eat as to catch.

There is no need, at this late point of the chapter, to say that there is no danger of the long summer day hanging heavily on one's hands, for the day's duties are by no means few or quickly accomplished. To catch fish enough to feed half a dozen sea-shore appetites three times a day is, of itself, no light task, to say nothing about cooking them. Then there is drift-wood to collect, and bait to find, and new places about the camp to explore, and at least two baths a day to take; so there is not so much time as might at first be imagined for dignified leisure, or for stretching ourselves, like Turkish sultans, on the divans — otherwise called army blankets — of our tent.

The daily bath is, of course, one of the greatest institutions of our life on the beach; and of all kinds of baths, we give the preference to those taken from the rocks at high tide.

Talk about moral courage! We will trust that man on any battle-field, who will sit quietly on a rock, and let the first big wave dash over him, on a coolish day, when the water, fresh from the open sea, seems to be miraculously preserved from freezing at a temperature far below 32° Fahrenheit, and when every breath of spray that blows against him feels like a blast from the North Pole. It is amusing to watch men who have only the ordinary supply of fortitude in such a place.

After the process of disrobing has been accomplished, and the fantastic livery which Neptune prescribes for his receptions has been donned, the average man will dance about upon the rocks for an unnecessarily long time, as though this were a most important preliminary to a bath. Then he will place one foot daintily in the water, and quickly draw it back, with a sudden jerk, that nothing but a severe bite from a gallinipper can satisfactorily explain.

This operation will be repeated a dozen times, more or less, until, apparently ashamed of himself, he takes his seat on a projecting ledge of rock, which the incoming tide has reached, to wait for the next wave, with a resolute look on his face, which plainly says, "I won't budge this time any way." Now he sees it coming, a quarter of a mile off—the monster which is to swallow him up if he keeps his seat. As the wave approaches, the courage oozes out at his fingers' ends, and the resolute look begins slowly to fade from his face, until, just at the critical moment when the water is about to dash over him with an angry swash, up he jumps, and is high and dry on the bank above before the wave breaks upon his rock.

However, after one has once been thoroughly wet down, one's courage to embrace the next wave is greatly increased, and each new billow is received with much laughter and many shivering, chattering shouts of welcome by the bathers.

And now, what more need we say? You

know where to go, what to do, and how to do it; and when we add, that all this, at a careful estimate, may be enjoyed for five dollars per week, we think it would be a clear waste of printer's ink and your time to add another page to this chapter.

CHAPTER V. *

DOWN EAST. — ST. JOHN. — PRINCE EDWARD ISLAND. — CAPE BRETON. — HALIFAX.

IN spite of the comfortable satisfaction one feels at having given good advice, it is hardly to be supposed that our counsel has been so generally followed, that all readers, who are pondering how they will pass their vacation, have either ordered their mountain outfit, or picked out a camping-ground at the sea-shore, or decided to take the next train for the Dominion. To all who are still undecided we assume the liberty of putting a few catechetical questions.

Is there at least one month of the twelve when

* The substance of a part of this chapter appeared in a series of letters written by the author, in the summer of 1872, to the Boston Daily Globe and to the Congregationalist.

it is your chief end and aim to keep cool? Then, "Young Man, go East,"— go to the Maritime Provinces.

Have you about a hundred dollars to spend on your summer vacation? There is no place where it will go farther, or do you more good, than in these same sea-coast dominions of **Her Majesty**.

Have you an eye for the beautiful in inanimate nature, and for the simple and unassuming in human nature? Nowhere can you find these qualities in greater perfection than among the fertile plains of Prince Edward Island, or the rugged high lands of Cape Breton.

Nothing better in the way of a summer climate could any one want, than he will find throughout this whole region. Here, for weeks at a time, the thermometer never rises to a too dizzy altitude; the sun's heat is grateful at midday, and no longer will you sigh for an abode in an ice-house, or for a lodge in some vast wilderness.

Is not this a delightful state of things, and

would not you enjoy them? Yea, verily; then meet us one of these bright mornings at the end of Commercial Wharf, in the good city of Boston, and with a St. John ticket in our pocket, and the smallest possible amount of baggage in our hand, we will step aboard the " New York " or " City of Portland," of the International Line.

As the clock strikes eight, the whistle shrieks, the cables are loosed, demonstrative Bluenoses give their departing friends a hasty embrace, the gangways are hauled in; the vessel quivers, throbs, and heaves; the wheel revolves, and — off we are, steaming through the shipping of the harbor.

There is one commodity which travellers " Down East," and, for that matter, the world over, we suppose, are very apt to forget to include in their list of indispensables when about to leave home. Yet this is more necessary to one's own comfort than the tooth-brush or the razor; and if one of a company has forgotten to take it with him, all the rest lose an appreciable proportion of their power of full enjoyment. The aforesaid article is a *settled purpose to be pleased with whatever one sees.*

As the spires and chimneys of Boston fade away in the distance, one should leave among them the idea (though it may require the greatest mental effort of which the traveller is capable) that the Old Bay State and her sister commonwealths are the only really desirable places on the face of the globe.

He should not find fault with "this confounded fog," or "that wretched rain," which is expected to-morrow, or with the "dreary shores of that barren province;" but he should call the fog "invigorating, if it is a little moist," the rocky bluffs of the New Brunswick shore, surmounted by stunted pine trees, "grand and imposing;" the Dolly Varden light-houses, built of alternate layers of red and white bricks, "picturesque;" and the occasional little beach of sand, with the fishers' white houses near by, and the green fields stretching far in beyond, "lovely and charming."

But though fault-finding and complaint are

to be repressed, don't suppose that we are about to waste any sickly sentimentality upon " the sea, the sea, the deep blue sea," or " life on the ocean wave," and all that sort of thing.

" Life on the ocean wave " may be a very nice affair when enclosed by the sides of a music-rack, and no sort of objection can be made to " the deep blue sea," when you view it from *terra firma*, with one of the good, old, everlasting rocks under your feet; but a different sort of a thing altogether is it when you view those same blue waves from the steamer's deck, caring not a copper whether you are above or below them — afraid that you will die during the first hour, and equally afraid during the second that you will not.

If you have a deadly enemy upon whom you wish to be revenged, just prevail upon him to go aboard of some ocean steamer; and then, during the first chopping sea, while he is leaning over the quarter-rail, gazing intently upon those " deep blue waves," or pretending that the lemon he holds in his hand is the most delicious of fruits, just ask him how he enjoys "life on the ocean wave."

All this by the way, however.

An eight hours' sail from Boston brings us to Portland, and as the steamer lies here for an hour or two, there is ample opportunity to get a glimpse of the fine buildings, and broad, tree-lined avenues, of this handsome "Forest City."

Eastport, the next stopping-place, — a town, situated near the entrance of Passamaquoddy Bay, — is much frequented by summer visitors. The waters of the adjacent bay afford fine opportunities for yachting and fishing. Directly across the harbor, within the limits of the Dominion of Canada, lies the interesting Island of Campobello, a favorite resort for sailing and chowder parties.

The afternoon's sail will be delightful by the red rocks of the New Brunswick coast, rising sheer out of the water from fifty to two hundred feet.

On the whole, however, the bold, rocky shores,

worn smooth by the continual dashing of white waves, and crowned with low pine trees, make one's first impression of New Brunswick grand and picturesque, rather than beautiful.

But St. John harbor, which is reached about sunset, makes up for all the loveliness we have lacked before; for nothing can be more charming than the islands and shores clad in emerald green, with the city sitting regally on a bluff that rises directly out of the water on one side, and the smiling slopes of Carleton on the other, while the multitude of fishing-boats and larger craft give an air of life and animation to the scene.

Even the model tourist, who is conscientiously determined to be pleased with whatever he sees, will be a little disappointed with the city of St. John; for, with cities as with men, the gods never bestow all their blessings upon the same individual. And St. John, though unrivalled in situation, presents a half-baked, unfinished, shiftless appearance, which is hardly pleasing to the eyes of a Yankee visitor.

The streets, though wide and regular, are not well paved, and are not paved at all for the most part; the houses, principally of wood, are of a uniform sombre brown color, which gives a dingy appearance to the whole place, and there are no buildings of particular beauty.

To this last statement, however, the Victoria Hotel, and two or three private residences on the west side of the city, form pleasing exceptions.

Nevertheless the St. Johnnies are very proud of their city, the fourth in size in the Dominion, and justly so too; for what constitutes a pleasant city? Not showy buildings and well-paved streets alone, by any means; but a pleasant and healthful climate, "first chop" scenery, as Sam Slick would say, abundant and cheap markets, and hospitable inhabitants; all which advantages St. John possesses in full measure.

One is struck, on first walking up from the wharf, by the great number of the smallest of hotels that are to be seen, each burdened with a ridiculously high-sounding name. Thus, here is a shabby wooden building, with three or four windows on each story, which a flaming sign over the door informs us is the " Grand International Hotel." That little martin-box on the right is the " Revere," perchance, and the one on the other side of the street is the " Royal Castle House."

The interior of these hotels, however, belies their sign-boards less than the exterior, and by the time we sit down to the bountiful table which the attentive landlord will spread for us, we shall begin to think that the name was not so ill chosen, after all.

But to be a little more explicit in regard to our hotel: the choice lies between the Victoria House (which is the only first-class house in the city, according to Boston notions, and where the charges are three dollars per day) and any one of the numerous third, fourth, fifth, down to fifteenth-class houses with which the city abounds.

We can recommend the Grand Central Hotel, the American House, or the Waverley House, as furnishing very tolerable accommodations at a moderate price — one dollar and fifty cents *per diem* we believe.

With the exception of one or two streets, the buildings are principally of wood, and a few hours of a Chicago or Boston fire would lay the whole city in ashes. A descendant of Ham, of whom inquiry was made for a sightly place to view the city, replied, with a royal flourish of his ebony palms, "Jest go up onto this yar bluff, and you will see de whole combustible." Our sable friend, in his desire for a long word, used one that applies to St. John better, probably, than he was aware.

The people of St. John, as well as all whom we shall see throughout the province, impress one very favorably. A healthier, ruddier set of men are not to be found on this footstool, and, as Dr. Lewis would say, their digestion being good, and their health perfect, we find them always ready to answer the thousand questions which a stranger is moved to ask.

No sweltering days and moist, sticky, unrestful nights do we here experience; but, as an intelligent knight of the hod assured us, "Ye may walk the strates all day and not sweat a drop, and at night, bedad, ye will feel the good of the clothes!"

The air, too, is remarkably invigorating — just warm enough, just cool enough; and a sea breeze is blowing at all times of day, the city being almost surrounded by the ocean.

To reach Shediac, which is something like a hundred miles from St. John, we take the European and North American Railway, and are whirled through the very heart of New Brunswick, along the coast of the Bay of Fundy. Past snug farm-houses and rich farms the track leads us; past the silvery lake near Claremont, where the great international rowing race took place — a race which proved to be the last for poor Renforth; and our time-table says that we are borne through villages bearing the euphonious names of Quispanisis, Passekeag, Apohaqui, Plumweseep, and Anagance. But further deponent saith not, except that all these much-named towns present a singular though hardly pleasing uniformity, since they invariably consist of a good station, a wretched grocery store and groggery combined, and an extensive mud-puddle.

Moncton, one of the largest towns on our route, contains some fine railroad repair-shops, and some unusually extensive mud-puddles, which would seem to render gondolas indispensable. Years ago Moncton was a town of considerable importance, being at the head of the main branch of the Bay of Fundy; but for many years past Father Time has done pretty much as he pleased with the old town, rotting a house here and another there, tumbling down this wall and starting a growth of weeds and grass in that street, until we could easily have imagined it to be the veritable deserted village of which the poet sung. Very recently, however, the iron road, that great energizer of the modern world, has begun to put new life into the grass-grown streets and moss-grown houses, and the town is quite renewing her youth.

At Moncton we leave the valley of the Bay of

Fundy, and strike across the country towards the Straits of Northumberland. This is, therefore, a favorable opportunity to refer briefly to the wonderful tides in the bay. The flood tides here sometimes take the very rare and terrible form of the " bore " — a great, perpendicular wall of water rushing up the bay, passing diagonally from side to side, and overwhelming everything in its path.

Imagine the stranger who might happen to be walking in the dry bed of the bay just before the coming of the " bore," roused from his reverie upon mud, muscles, and clams, whose happiness at high water is always such an appropriate and convenient simile, by a mighty, rushing, gurgling roar in the far distance.

Instantly a graphic picture of his younger days will come to his mind, representing a distressed looking Pharaoh, surrounded by a few wretched followers, standing upon the topmost point of a very sharp rock, in the midst of some extraordinary looking waves, while a row of jolly Israelites are grinning at them from the safe bank of the other side; and he will imagine that he hears a chorus of Jubilee Singers on the bank above him, chanting, —

"To drown old Pharo's army, hallelujah,
To drown old Pharo's army, hallelu."

But he must dismiss both Pharaoh's army and the Jubilee Singers from his thoughts, and run for his life, for the roar which he hears in the distance proceeds from the "bore," ten feet high (if it happens to be at the time of spring tide), coming towards him at the rate of twelve miles an hour, and bringing sure destruction to man, or beast, or boat, that may be in its way. The tide rises thirty feet here, — not so high by half as at some other parts of the bay, — and the wave which leads the van is the only remarkable one, the others being scarcely a tenth of its size.

Shediac is reached soon after we start from Moncton station, and here we leave the train. The European and North American runs two miles farther, and ends at the coast, at a little place called Point du Chêne. But may you not, my reader, be obliged to tarry long at Shediac, waiting for the Prince Edward Island boat, for this is, without doubt, one of the most slipshod places to be found on our little planet.

Do you wish for a minute description of this lovely retreat? Take the most wretched New England village, of about seventy-five houses, to be found in either of our six Puritanic commonwealths; bring all the two-story houses to the level of cottages; tear off every blind in the place; paint all the houses a dingy color; turn every store and shop, where a scrap of reading matter can be bought, into a grocery and groggery; dig cradle-holes in all the roads large enough to bury the horse and buggy with which you jolt over them; level all the hills within twenty miles; cut down half of the forest trees, and turn the rest into stunted spruces; metamorphose all the fields and pastures into bogs and swamps; and run a muddy bay, with a muddier shore, along one side of the town, and you have a twin Shediac in Massachusetts, which it would be hard to distinguished from the New Brunswick original.

But even Shediac has its redeeming qualities; for, as is the case with all these provincial sea-coast towns, in the way of climate nothing better could be desired. The air, always cool and fresh, has a certain invigorating quality which turns the blue of one's mental firmament into the rosiest colors (if one lives here long enough, the blue is all driven to the nose), and it is said to be impossible for a hypochondriac to live within a dozen miles of the place.

Besides its climate, Shediac can boast of a large saw-mill, which turns out six million feet of lumber during the three months of the year it is in operation.

Here a log is taken in the rough, and by the aid of a gang-saw to cut it into the right thicknesses, and a circular saw to trim off the edges, in an incredibly short time the sturdy pine trunk is transformed into planks or boards, ready to be shipped to Europe. Four hundred logs a day take the shape of building material in this one mill, and many other mills along the coast turn out an equal amount of lumber, all of which is shipped directly to European ports.

The two churches of the place may also be ranked among its redeeming features, for they are neat, attractive buildings, which would be a disgrace to no village in the land.

They have a novel method, however, of calling people to the sanctuary in Shediac. When the appointed time arrives, a small boy with a huge dinner-bell mounts the topmost step, and by shaking his bell, proclaims to all within hearing that divine service is about to begin. Doubtless this method answers every purpose, though the effect is hardly soul-inspiring, since it is more likely to lead one to reflect upon his gastronomic wants, than his spiritual necessities.

The inhabitants of Shediac, like most people in the province, are free and open-hearted, polite to strangers, and proud of their native town and country.

To them no land is equal to the fields and

meadows of New Brunswick; their row of straggling houses is a "thriving village," and the little stretch of mud and sand is a "lovely beach." For dwellers in such a place this blissful contentment is invaluable. May you ever, dear New Brunswickans, continue to jolt over your wretched highways with the same self-satisfied faces that you now wear!

But whatever day of the week we reach Shediac, Tuesday or Friday morning will at length come round, and bring with it one of the Prince Edward Island steamers, to transport us from the dreary wastes which surround Shediac to that lovely isle which long ago received the name of the old Duke of Kent — Prince Edward.

A perfect gem is this island, — a beautiful emerald, the largest and brightest of all the jewels which adorn the bosom of the great gulf.

Do not smile at this enthusiastic statement, for it is strictly true, as every traveller will vote when steaming up to the Summerside Wharf, and seeing the long reaches of green fields on either side, without a rock, or cliff, or withered pasture, to mar the quiet loveliness of the scene. There are sixty miles of coast of the same character, which the eye cannot reach, stretching away on either side.

Neither does distance, by any means, lend all the enchantment to the view, for when we land from the steamer and take the coach, fields of the same unrivalled green will meet our eye, throughout the length and breadth of the island, and we exclaim, " O for perpetual summer, to make Prince Edward Island the paradise of the globe!"

But, alas! our wish is far from granted, for throughout more than seven months of the year the frost king holds undisputed sway, and our charming isle is as dreary and prosaic as can well be imagined.

Even in summer the occasional evidences of man's hand would remind one that he is still on this mundane sphere, while at the same time, from the style of architecture of severe simplicity.

which the natives have adopted in building their houses, one is led to think that, in their opinion, at least, the island is beautiful enough already, without any effort on their part to improve it.

Summerside, where we land, is a more forsaken place even than Shediac; and if we stay but a short time, the only remembrance of the town we shall carry away, will be of a row of extraordinarily mean-looking houses, planted helter-skelter in the midst of a great pasture of live stock, composed of equal parts of scurvy dogs, draggled geese, and dirty children.

Bagnall's coach for Charlottetown, however, will take us out of the vicinity of Summerside at an early hour. The ride will well repay us for rising at the first call of the blue-bird, for though Mr. Bagnall's coaches are hardly first class, we shall find much to interest us in this forty miles. The first thing that strikes the eye is the uniform excellence of the hay-fields. No starveling patches of clover do we see, and spindling crops of grass, where each individual Timothy Grass seems afraid of his next neighbor, and tries to keep at a respectful distance; but broad acres of the stoutest grass, red with clover blossoms, or waving like a wheat-field, with the full heads of timothy or herds-grass. The fields of potatoes, too, white with blossoms, if it is late in the summer, it would be hard to beat, even in that land of murphies — the Emerald Isle.

Oats, also, do remarkably well in the light, red loam which forms the inland soil; and barley and rye, as well as most of the hardier vegetables, are raised to a considerable extent.

The three months of warm weather which the province enjoys hardly gives the corn time to ripen; and the only field of corn which we ever saw on the island, had, when about a foot high, made a sickly attempt to tassel out, but had signally failed.

There are scarcely any stones on the island; the few that are to be found are a soft, friable sandstone, which seems in a hurry to crumble back to sand again, and leave the soil wholly free from any impediment to the farmer's plough. The inhabitants here have a curious way, we shall notice, of economizing their few precious stones in building roadside walls. First they lay a course of pebbles, then a thick layer of sod, then another course of pebbles, another layer of sod, and so on, until they have made a stout and quite durable wall, out of sods and small stones, which our farmers would consider worthless for such a purpose.

Other things which will strike one as curious are the little barns with movable roofs, which are to be seen on every side. Instead of having one or two large barns, the islanders have several, perhaps many small ones. These are walled up to the height of ten feet or so, and above the walls extend four uprights as much higher. Through a hole in each corner of the roof these uprights are placed, and upon them the roof slides up or down, always resting on the hay underneath. Thus, in the fall of the year, a stranger, by simply glancing at the barns on the road-side, could tell whether it was a year of plenty or a season of scarcity; for if " the labor of the husbandman had been blessed," as the Thanksgiving proclamations say, the little roof will be raised to the topmost notch, and the barns will be bursting out with plenty; but if Jack Frost comes too early and nips the crop, the roofs of the barns will proclaim it by resting flat upon the walls, while the long posts stretch gaunt and bare above them.

If we go out to ride, we shall find that, "turn out to the *left*, as the law directs," is the rule here, and a most perplexing rule for a Yankee to drive by it is, too; and we shall have many narrow escapes from collision with the decidedly antiquated and rickety teams of the people of the land.

Our text-books on natural history are faulty in one respect; not one of them contains the following passage: —

"What creatures besides antelopes are noted for their wonderful curiosity?"

"*Ans*. The inhabitants of some of the smaller Provincial towns."

When the stranger first enters one of these villages, he is surprised to see every doorway, and window, and street corner crowded with men, women, and children, whose sole purpose in life seems to be to gaze upon his form and features. The emotions of this stranger will be various. First, the thought flits through his mind that this is a village of detectives, and that he is suspected of some great crime, on which account each of the inhabitants is mentally taking his photograph and exact measurements.

But the idea is so preposterous that even the infants in arms should belong to the detective corps, that he soon abandons this notion, and emotions of pleasure take its place. "Ah," says he to himself, "I must have become very distinguished since I left home; received the nomination for governor or congressman, perhaps, or at least 'alderman of my native town.' Who knows? And though I have not heard of it myself, it has got to the ears of these good people, and they take this method of showing their approbation. But it is very singular," he thinks, "that they utter no word, neither give vent to their feelings in a single cheer;" and about this time, his joy gives place to terror and dismay, as he thinks, "What is the matter with my face or figure? Are my feet turning into hoofs, or my ears into horns? Is my skin becoming black, or is there a great rent in the back of my coat?"

And he rushes home, and to his looking-glass, in great anxiety, to find his personal appearance unchanged, and to anathematize the stupid curiosity of the natives.

But this trait is not characteristic of all the people of the provinces, by any means; it appears only in a few less favored regions; for in general the people are as polite, genial, and hospitable as any one could wish. Indeed, it is said that on Prince Edward Island the belated traveller will find at any farm-house, when night overtakes him, food and bed of the best quality, for which the good farmer feels insulted to be offered pay.

But we were just starting out from Summerside, at five o'clock in the morning. Soon we reach "Hazel Grove," as Farmer Bagnall calls his half-way house, between Summerside and

Charlottetown; and while we are waiting to have our horses changed, we may as well step inside and partake of a first-class breakfast of salmon or mackerel, lobsters, mutton (the island is noted for its fine mutton), and cold beef, with their usual concomitants, for all of which the modest sum of twenty-five cents is considered a full equivalent.

Moreover, we must not fail to visit Mrs. Bagnall's fragrant dairy, and her fine kitchen garden, which is quite a marvel for these cold northern latitudes.

If it is as late as the middle of August, she will point out, with evident pride, her rows of "early green peas," just beginning to fill out.

Early green peas in the middle of August; think of that, ye Massachusetts farmers, whose dry pea-vines hang at that time, sear and yellow, on rustling bushes!

We would suggest to any devoted lover of early fruits and vegetables, that he might greatly prolong his enjoyment by following the seasons along as it were, by travelling through various climes. For instance, starting in the tropics in the month of March, he might enjoy his strawberries and cherries, green peas and asparagus, during the very first days of spring. Then he would slowly journey to more temperate climes, keeping pace with the northward progress of his favorite dishes, until at length, the first part of autumn would find him eating strawberries and green peas in Mrs. Bagnall's garden, at Hazel Grove.

Twenty miles of stage-coach ride from Hazel Grove brings us to Charlottetown, the capital and largest city of the island; and quite pleased shall we be with the appearance of the place. Ten thousand people, living for the most part in low, brown, wooden houses, arranged on wide and regular streets, compose the population of this very quiet, orderly city.

The commerce of Charlottetown is already considerable, and the excellent harbor will admit of a great metropolis on this Island of Prince Edward, should the great trade-winds ever blow strongly in this direction.

Though Charlottetown can boast of but few fine buildings, yet she possesses two or three fine government houses. They are built of brown sandstone, brought at great expense from New Brunswick, and, standing in the principal square, are a great ornament to the place. The great want of the city is good hotel accommodations. The public houses are all small, the tables rather poor, and all are so much alike that it will be of little use to mention the names of any.

The school system of the island appears to be in rather a primitive state, though the schoolhouses along the road much resemble (in all respects but their shingled sides and their lack of paint) the corresponding nurseries for young ideas in New Hampshire and Vermont. One is in no danger of forgetting, however, that he is no longer in the land of Young America, when, as he rides by, he sees the rows of school boys and girls drawn up on both sides of the road, respectfully pulling their forelocks, and dropping courtesies to the passing stranger.

We are told that the school-mistresses, who instil ideas of politeness and of the alphabet into the young islanders, receive forty pounds a year for their services, and doubtless deem themselves "passing rich" at that. "Forty pounds, or one hundred and thirty-two dollars," as one of them informed us.

From recollections of early school-days, and of the table of English money, we had always supposed that forty pounds was more than one hundred and thirty-two dollars, but surely, the "school-marm" ought to know.

Provisions are wonderfully cheap on this isle of plenty. To illustrate the low prices prevailing in these favored domains of royalty, let us suppose that we have gone to housekeeping here, and are about to sit down to a "good square meal," to fill up the vacancy which a long ride over the billowy roads of the island has left.

That plate of fresh salmon which first comes on has cost five cents per pound, if it is in the salmon season, while, if a fish of the species chosen to grace the Massachusetts Hall of Representatives, had been preferred, we might have bought a fifteen pounder for half as many coppers. Of course, since we are in the land of John Bull, we must not discard the national dish; and for that choice roast which next makes its appearance the price was ten cents per pound, while the mutton chop by its side cost us just half as much.

The chickens which flank the roast beef have cost thirty-two cents per pair; the eggs are twelve cents per dozen; the butter fifteen, and the cheese five, cents per pound.

Of course this is very extravagant; but, then, one must eat something, you know, even if he don't lay up a cent; and he may as well grow poor on such things as spend all his substance for fresh mackerel at thirty cents a dozen, or lobsters at a cent and a half apiece. Indeed, such privations in the line of fresh provisions do these poor islanders endure, that it has been thought best, in some quarters, to re-enact the old Connecticut law, that "no master mechanic shall give his apprentices fresh salmon to eat more than three times a week."

The small change with which pay is given for these necessaries of life is rather perplexing to eyes accustomed to greenback currency; for besides the dimes, half dimes, and quarters, whose Goddess of Liberty wears a strangely familiar expression, we are continually exercising our reckoning powers to ascertain the value of certain twenty, twenty-four, forty-eight, and sixty cent pieces, besides a liberal sprinkling of sixpences, shillings, and florins, bearing the queen's image and superscription; and occasionally the grouty visages of Georgius IV. or Gulielmus IV. find their way into our pocket-book, carrying with them far greater veneration than the memory of those royal personages themselves is likely to do.

On the whole, the people of Prince Edward, politically and socially, are very much like the rest of the great world about them. The men wrangle and grow furious over politics; the women gossip in the most approved fashion; and the young folks put on airs, and affectionately designate their "parients" as "paw," and "maw," just as though three thousand miles of ocean did not roll between them and London aristocracy.

While New Brunswick and Nova Scotia belonged to the Dominion of Canada from the beginning, Prince Edward Island long remained independent, exceedingly jealous of everything Canadian, and until very recently has been governed in all matters by Houses of Senators and Commons of its own.

This little province, too, of scarce a hundred thousand souls, has, according to its papers, a complete Tammany of its own, and its handful of legislators find it impossible to perform the functions of their office without expending several thousand dollars annually for pocket-knives, brandy, lead pencils at two dollars apiece, &c., if the opposition journals are to be believed. Base imitators these of our ignoble example!

A railroad (the first the province has ever had) has recently been constructed from Summerside to Charlottetown, and is now open for passenger traffic, we believe, so that in the future travellers will have a more speedy method of reaching the capital, if they choose to go by rail. Still, on a bright summer morning, for pure air, lovely scenery, and a pleasant glimpse of country life in the province, commend us to a top seat on one of Mr. Bagnall's coaches.

Rustico, a little village eighteen miles from Charlottetown, is where the people of "the city" rusticate, and it is almost the only watering-place on the island. The ride to Rustico and back will fill up one day of our stay at Charlottetown very pleasantly, and, if in the season, we can have rare sport with the flocks of snipe, ducks, and other waterfowl which here frequent the coast. One day, too, must be devoted to fishing, for famous are the trout brooks of Prince Edward's land.

For nearly half of the year communication between the island and main land is kept up with great difficulty and danger, for all the harbors are frozen over five feet thick or more; and very frequently the whole gulf, from shore to shore, is covered with ice. At such times the mails are transported on ice-boats, which are so constructed that they can be drawn over the ice or propelled through the water with equal facility. In summer, however, an excellent line of steamers plies between Charlottetown and the coast of New Brunswick and Nova Scotia; and if we have seen all that the time of our vacation allows of this Queen of the St. Lawrence Gulf, we will take the steamer St. Lawrence or the Princess of Wales for Cape Breton.

Our first stopping-place will be Pictou, a name connected, no doubt, in many of our minds, chiefly with the grimy coal-barges which frequent our harbors. Years ago, Pictou was a place of considerable importance, as the seat of an extensive lumber trade; but gradually the forests were cut off, lumber became scarce, and Pictou's glory seemed waning. About this time, however, rich deposits of coal were found in the neighborhood; and now the place is more flourishing than at first, and the fossilized forests of antediluvian days seem likely to be a more lasting benefit to the region than were the pine groves of the present century.

But we have hardly time to think of Pictou's varied fortunes, and to notice the fine Catholic church on the hill, — placed on the highest point of land, it is said, that the sailor, as he nears harbor, may first of all see its spire pointing heavenwards, — before the lines are cast off, the heavy walking-beam begins its regular march again, and we are headed for Port Hawksbury, in the Gut of Canso.

We should like to introduce our readers to Port Hawksbury, as we saw it for the first time one lovely August afternoon. The setting sun was just throwing his last horizontal rays straight through the gap which the Gut of Canso makes between Cape Breton and the main land of Nova Scotia. On the right towered the bristling heights of Cape Porcupine, while on the left stretched far away the bold and rugged scenery of Cape Breton.

The steamer seemed to be ploughing through liquid gold, instead of salt sea brine, and it required little imagination to lead to the idea that every turn of the strait would bring us to the entrance of some enchanted palace, or to some Sindbad's cave in the mountain side.

Soon we draw up to the Port Hawksbury wharf, and here we may as well dismiss all poetic notions, for a scene awaits us which we are sure has its match nowhere else on the globe.

Instead of the hospitable descendants of the English, whom we have seen heretofore, a crowd of brawny sons of Caledonia greet us, all clad in gray homespun, and chattering a most fearful language, which sounds like the roll of distant thunder, the crash of crockery, and the jabber of a dozen Dutchmen, all rolled into one.

To get a clearer idea of the scene, imagine half a hundred French Canadian teams (the most ancient of vehicles, and most bony of horses, like those which visit our New England villages each summer) collected into a small space near the wharf; then imagine each one of the Canuck owners of these turnouts shouting, and yelling, and pulling, and winking, and whispering to your individual self, to induce you to employ him to carry you to West Bay, thirteen miles distant, and you have some notion of the scene which greets the arrival of each steamer at the port.

First, a big Scotchman seizes you by the arm, as though he would carry you to West Bay bodily. Him you shake off with difficulty, when another son of Anak embraces you on the other side.

Over there stands a stout Jehu, who beckons and smiles in a most familiar way, after the "long-lost-brother" fashion, and you almost feel that it is a personal slight to neglect his entreaties.

Just behind him stands another, who winks at you in a confidential manner, as much as to say, "All these other chaps are impostors. I am the only regular, first-class wagon."

We choose the least importunate of our newly-made friends, and with many contortions of body and groanings of spirit, we stow ourselves away on the back seats, while the big Caledonian mounts in front.

Would you know the most approved method of riding over these mountain roads? Keep your eyes riveted on the road, about ten rods ahead of your Bucephalus; then, when you see that he is approaching a cradle-hole, large stone, or rickety bridge, shut your eyes, hold your breath, raise yourself about six inches from your seat, and try to lose your consciousness, until you get over the obstacle, and on the smooth ground beyond. To be sure, if you adopt this method, you will use your seats but very little; but then the effect is exhilarating, or exciting, to say the least, and on the whole these roads are excellent preventives of indigestion.

Whether the horses have no great expectations of oats awaiting them in the manger at home, or perhaps for some other reason, they are not very ambitious to get over the road, and it takes all the driver's powers of persuasion to keep them moving.

First, he encourages them by a long series of

clucks; then he varies the monotony by remarking, "Git up, g'long," several hundred times in no subdued tone; then he pours forth a large number of Gaelic expletives, and by this time is ready to return to the original clucks.

Feeling in a communicative mood, we attempt to carry on a conversation with him.

"Well, driver, do you ever see any game in these regions?"

"Yes (Git up; g'long; hi, there; gee, Buck; git up; g'long, g'long) — sometimes." And now follows half a page of horse talk, peculiar to Breton drivers, which can't possibly be written; and then we venture to ask, —

"What do you find to shoot, driver?"

"Pa'tridges (Git up; keep the road; g'long, there) — ducks" (now comes a prolonged hiss at the nigh horse), "rabbits, and you sometimes see — (Hi, there; what are you about, Charlie? git up, git up; g'long)." During a long list of Gaelic adjectives which follow, we rather lose the connection of his discourse, and he shouts out — "a bear"

"Where? where?" we excitedly cry, while the ladies of the party are preparing to faint, and things generally begin to look serious. But our driver continues to cluck calmly to his nags, and explains himself by remarking, "I only said (G'long, Buck; don't be lazy, Charlie), that I see a bear" — "Where is he?" we again demand; while the ladies entreat, "Do, dear Mr. Driver, please hurry on!" But our big Scotchman finishes his series of clucks before he does his sentence — "now and then in the woods."

We recognize the force of the old saying, that no man can do two things well at the same time, and conclude not to question our driver to any great extent during the rest of the ride.

At West Bay there is a little steamer ready to carry us to Sydney, a hundred and twenty miles distant; and after paying Jehu a dollar apiece, which he has fairly earned, we go on board, and are soon threading our way through the intricacies of the Bras d'Or.

And a wonderful inland sea is this Bras d'Or, — the Mediterranean of North America, — one hundred miles long, and from ten rods to ten miles wide. It extends throughout the entire length of Cape Breton, dividing the island into two peninsulas.

High mountains enclose the lake on all sides, sometimes rising abruptly from the water, — then twice viewed, once in the clear air above, and once in the blue depths beneath, — at other times tinged with blue by the distance, while between them and the water's bank are long slopes of cultivated land, dotted here and there with the white cottages of the farmers or fishermen.

The inhabitants of Cape Breton number about twenty-five thousand, and for the most part they are purely Scotch. In many places the people speak nothing but their native tongue, and the stranger finds it very difficult to understand or to be understood, as Gaelic is one of the most unspeakable languages in the world. Moreover, these Bretoners are a very primitive race in every sense of the word; tall, broad-shouldered, and muscular, they are clad almost universally in gray homespun, and live in the smallest of white-washed cottages. Their wants are supplied without difficulty, for a few acres of cultivated land give them plenty of oatmeal, and the Bras d'Or is filled with all varieties of fine fish, which may be very easily caught.

The Kirk of Scotland (Presbyterian) is the only church which flourishes among these people, and it is said that they still prefer sermons of two hours' length to any other.

As we steam along through the unruffled waters of the "Arm of Gold," far off there to the eastward we can just discern the marble mountain, whose white sides glisten afar in the sunlight. The marble, which is very fair, though not of the best quality, has not yet been quarried to any considerable extent.

Besides the marble mountain, the geologist finds many other objects of interest. One of these is the stratum of coal which underlies much of this island, and which is supposed to stretch in a continuous belt from Sydney to Pictou, a distance of a hundred and fifty miles. But especially will the geologist be interested in the numerous fossils to be found on these shores. Branches of trees he will find turned into the solid rock; stigmaria and sigillaria, with their bark and all their depressions and roughnesses as plainly visible as they were twenty thousand years ago; delicate ferns, and the skeletons of various leaves firmly embedded in the hard stone; and all these treasures, at which we usually gaze under the glass cases of a cabinet, to be had for nothing on the shores of Cape Breton.

The coal deposits of this region are really wonderful. Dig a few feet downwards in almost any place, and you will strike a rich seam of these black diamonds. In many spots along the shore, the earth having been washed away by the waves, the coal has fallen down upon the pebbly beach in considerable quantities, and is there collected by the inhabitants.

Many families, however, need not go even so far as this for their fuel, but, just stepping down cellar, they find a natural coal-bin, as inexhaustible as the widow's barrel of meal, all prepared for them. The coal is bituminous, and not the best for family use, but excellent for steam-producing purposes.

The entrance to the Bras d'Or from the Gulf of St. Lawrence is one of the most remarkable features of this inland sea. For nearly two miles we steam through a narrow and tortuous pass, along which only a steamer of very small dimensions can make its way, and throughout the whole distance we could almost jump from our little craft to the shore of either peninsula of Cape Breton. A beautiful sail is this through the "narrows;" the strait seems to open a passage for the prow as we go on, until the white breakers and dashing waves proclaim that we are out once more in the great gulf.

On either side of the outer entrance of the Bras d'Or tower rocky headlands, which, at a little distance, much resemble fortresses. Half a dozen guns and a company of regulars would make them so in good earnest.

Thirteen miles by water from these natural forts, is Sydney, the former capital, and at present the largest city of Cape Breton.

The city is notable for nothing except a look of quiet decay, and some very fine piers, from which immense quantities of coal are annually shipped.

The coal mines are some three or four miles from the city, and their vast, sunless depths, running out for two miles under the ocean's waves; their long, wide seams of coal; their human inhabitants, whose coal-begrimed faces give them a very sinister expression; and their plump little horses, which have never seen a ray of daylight, — make them well worth a visit from any traveller in Cape Breton.

North Sydney is a place of more commercial importance than old Sydney, and in its well-situated harbor can be seen every sort of craft from the ugliest of little coal barges to the trimmest of British frigates.

Old Louisburg Fort, some twenty-four miles from Sydney, on the south side of the island, should be visited if there is time, for this old French capital was long the bloody battle-ground of the French and English when they fought for the possession of this region. Little but historic memories is left to old Louisburg now, however, for, with the exception of a few fishermen's huts, the place is well nigh deserted.

While stopping at Sydney, we must make Mrs. Herns's our headquarters, if that good lady has a spare room for us, for at most of the so-called hotels of Sydney we should fare but poorly.

Now the northern limit of our vacation journey has been reached, and if we wish to make the tour of the maritime provinces complete, we shall doubtless retrace our steps as far as Pictou, then strike across Nova Scotia by rail, and return to our republican home by way of Halifax.

On the return journey, we reach Port Hawksbury at nightfall, and going to bed in the steamer as she lies at the wharf, awake the next morning within sight of Pictou.

The steward hurries breakfast, the passengers hurry down their salmon and beefsteak, and then hurry ashore as the steamer grazes the Pictou wharf. But here all haste ceases, for Pictou, like every other Acadian village, always preserves its unruffled equanimity, and you might as well try to hasten the growth of the forests primeval as to hurry the Bluenose inhabitants of this region.

Before a great while, however, we are flying over the Nova Scotia Railway, which takes the traveller from Pictou to Halifax, through a country wonderful for its rocks and barrenness, and for little else, apparently. To be sure, in the neighborhood of Truro there are many fine farms and stout fields of grass and grain, but throughout most of the journey the eye rests upon nothing but wide pastures, whose only crops are huge boulders, swampy lowlands covered with stunted brushwood, and forests of pine and spruce, through which numerous fires have raged, leaving the trees leafless and dry.

But the very headquarters and capital of this region, as far as barrenness goes, is in the neighborhood of Windsor Junction, where the Annapolis valley road joins the Nova Scotia Railway.

Here, for miles and miles, scarcely a foot of soft earth can be found. Stones, rocks, boulders, ledges, everywhere meet the eye. Every house is literally founded upon a rock.

The man who finds sermons in stones ought to spend all his Sundays here; and should he be of a religious turn of mind, and live to be as old as Methuselah, he never need hear the same discourse repeated.

Fancy the top of Mount Washington brought down to the level of the sea, and suppose the rocks, instead of being heaped together in a romantic sort of way, as rocks always should be, spread out very thickly over several square miles of territory, and you have a faint idea of the appearance of Windsor Junction and the surrounding country.

There is an ancient tradition in this region accounting for this stony ground, which runs something as follows: —

When Pyrrha and Deucalion passed this way, they engaged in their customary occupation of throwing boulders over their heads. But the rocks, partaking of the universal sluggish and tardy habits of the country, thought there was no hurry about turning into flesh and blood, and so waited until the second father and mother of mankind had got out of sight, when it was no longer possible for them to take the human shape divine; and ever since they have remained weighty monuments to the evils of procrastination.

By taking the Annapolis Railway, a few miles of travel will bring us right to the home of Evangeline. For here, —

"In the Acadian land, on the shores of the Basin of
    Minas,
Distant, secluded, still, the little village of Grand-Pré
Lay in the fruitful valley. Vast meadows stretched to
    the eastward,
Giving the village its name, and pasture to flocks with-
    out number;
There, in the midst of its farms, reposed the Acadian
    village.
Strongly built were the houses, with frames of oak and
    of chestnut,
Such as the peasants of Normandy built in the reign
    of the Henries.

"Thatched were the roofs, with dormer windows; and
    gables, projecting
Over the basement below, protected and shaded the
    doorways."

But though the Basin of Minas is just as fruitful as ever, not quite so secluded and still is the Acadian village as when Benedict Bellefontaine dwelt on his goodly acres. For modern life and bustle have even reached the Basin of Minas; the iron horse snorts under the very dormer windows and gables projecting, and the conductor sticks his head into the car, and cries out, " Grand Pree," in the broadest of Saxon accents. Still in company with our pocket Longfellows, we can spend many enjoyable hours in this Annapolis valley.

After leaving Windsor Junction, the Nova Scotia road runs on the ram's horn principle for thirteen miles, when it finds its terminus in the station at Halifax.

But we are still two miles and a half from the business portion of the city, and must take one of the little horse cars which are furnished with only one door, and that one in front, and ride to the " International," or " Halifax," or " Acadian," as fortune may direct.

The fickle goddess once took us to the first-mentioned house; and if we remember aright, we found no occasion to wish for a change, though we have no doubt that either of the others is equally good.

Halifax impresses the stranger much more favorably than any other city in this part of Her Majesty's dominions, Mr. Warner to the contrary, notwithstanding. It has neither the unfinished, unsubstantial appearance of St. John, nor the straggling look of most of the smaller towns of the province. To be sure, a fresh coat of paint, of some other color than dirty brown, would greatly improve many of the houses even of Halifax; but for the most part, the principal streets are lined with substantial blocks of brick or brown stone.

From the Citadel there is a fine view of the beautiful site of the city, its many church-spires and fine school-houses, its spacious harbor white with the sails of many nations, and the broad Atlantic, with its waves and breakers rolling beyond.

The city is remarkably well protected, for, besides the bristling Citadel, there is Fort George in the harbor, flanked on either side by Fort Clarence and the Eastern Battery, ready to belch out fire and lead from a hundred mouths.

If possible, we must be in Halifax during one of the market days. These come every Wednesday and Saturday, and then the market streets of the city present a very striking appearance. From early morn the little country carts begin to pour into the city, loaded with a very small portion of everything which the eye of man ever rested upon.

The owners of these treasures arrange their teams near the market, until every street and alley within a radius of half a mile is lined with them. Here is a little go-cart with a small bunch of tansy, a few strips of slippery elm, and a half dozen quarts of diminutive green cranberries, for its freight; there stands another loaded with a few clusters of bunchberries, as many stalks of rhubarb, and a little watercress.

In this corner, a family of Micmac Indians are fashioning rainbow-colored baskets, and at the same time nursing several bronze-faced little pappooses, which are curiously cradled between two flat pieces of board. On that side, a number of shiny-faced colored sisters are dispensing pop beer, greasy doughnuts, and gingerbread men to numerous cannibal little boys and girls who have come in with their parents from the country. Here an auctioneer is cracking his voice in the vain effort to sell some chairs and tables that have outlived their usefulness, while his stentorian tones are almost drowned by the quacking of ducks and the squawking of chickens, which are tied by their legs and thrown together in a heap on one side, to await the coming of a purchaser.

White men, black men, red men, Scotchmen, Frenchmen, Yankees, and Bluenoses; jabbering English, Gaelic, Micmac, and darky lingo, bantering and haggling in a way that is known only in Halifax on a market day.

Dalhousie College is one of the institutions of Halifax. The exterior of the single college building, to be sure, does not speak very well for the higher educational advantages of Nova Scotia; but it may be presumed that the faculty and curriculum do not at all correspond to the building.

In one of the chairs of the college — we think of moral philosophy — sits Professor De Mille, of novelistic fame.

It seems almost ridiculous to think of the author of the rollicking " Dodge Club," the jolly " Lady of the Ice," and the mysterious " Cryptogram " drilling Butler and metaphysics into a parcel of college boys; nevertheless it is said that this many-sided professor excels in morals as well as in tragic love-scenes.

Dartmouth is the principal suburb of Halifax, where a large skate factory and an immense ropewalk are situated. But the place is of little interest, and will hardly repay a visit.

To complete the circle of our provincial tour we must take one of the steamers of the Boston, Halifax and Prince Edward Island Steamship

Line, or, if we choose, the Falmouth, which will land us at Portland.

Or, if the traveller wishes to see one of the most interesting sections of Nova Scotia, he can return by way of the Windsor and Annapolis Railway and the Bay of Fundy steamer, returning thence to the United States the way he came. For a part of the distance to the junction, this is retracing our steps; but having reached the Basin of Minas, the road runs along near the southern shore of the Bay of Fundy. The broad marshes along the way are protected by dikes, built by the old Acadian French settlers. The view on the right reaches to the bay and the hills of Parrsboro', on the opposite shore. The bold promontory of Cape Blomidon is a prominent object in the landscape. We pass Hantsport, a busy ship-building village; Wolfville, where is Acadia College; and Kentsville, where the railway offices are located, and reach Annapolis, the terminus. This is the ancient Port Royal, the first capital of the province, and one of the oldest places on the continent. The remains of old fortifications are still standing, and from the summit can be had fine views of the river and the surrounding country.

On being transferred to the steamer Empress, the traveller passes down the deep Annapolis basin, with a range of high hills on either side, to Digby, where a landing is made. This quiet, shady town has a pleasant outlook from the hill-side. The opening from the basin is between high bluffs, and through this the steamer passes into the Bay of Fundy, and after a run of three or four hours makes a landing at the wharf in St. John.

In this schedule we start from Boston and come back to the Tri-Mountain City.

From Boston to St. John *via* International Line of steamers,	$5.50
Grand Central Hotel at St. John, two days, at $1.50 per day,	3.00
From St. John to Shediac *via* European and North American Railroad,	2.50
Weldon House at Shediac, one day, at $1.00 per day,	1.00
From Shediac to Summerside, Prince Edward Island steamers,	1.50

From Summerside to Charlottetown *via* Bagnall's stage,	1.50
Hotel bill at Charlottetown, four days,	6.00
From Charlottetown to Port Hawkesbury, Prince Edward Island steamers,	4.00
From Port Hawkesbury to West Bay, by coach,	1.00
From West Bay to Sydney,	3.00
At Mrs. Herns's, Sydney, three days,	3.00
Fares back to Pictou, over same route,	6.00
From Pictou to Halifax, N. S., railroad,	3.25
At International Hotel, Halifax, four days,	6.00
From Halifax to Boston *via* Boston, Halifax and Prince Edward Island Steamship Line,	9.00
Estimate for incidental expenses, including discount on money, &c., &c.,	40.00
Total expense for round trip,	$96.25

For those wishing to get a glimpse of the maritime provinces, a refreshing sea voyage, and at the same time not wishing to spend as much time or money as the trip we have just described requires, we can recommend nothing pleasanter than to take the round trip with one of the steamers of the Boston, Halifax and Prince Edward Island Steamship Line.

The steamships of this company, the Carroll

and Alhambra, are safe, roomy, and fast vessels, of some fourteen hundred tons burden, well furnished and well officered in every particular.

The state-rooms are all double, and supplied with life-preserving mattresses, capable of outriding any storm if it should be our bad luck to take a compulsory voyage on one of them.

If we decide to follow the fortunes of the steamers on one of their trips, some Saturday noon will find us steaming away from Boston from the end of T Wharf, and, wind and weather permitting, the next Monday morning will find us safely anchored in the snug harbor of Halifax.

Our steamer only remains here a few hours, but long enough to give a very fair idea of this aristocratic little metropolis. Then we are on our way again, skirting the Nova Scotia coast, and getting our fill of the glorious views which the Straits of Canso afford by the early daylight of the next morning.

Port Hawkesbury, which we reached before from the other end of the strait, is excited by the arrival of the Boston steamer early this Tuesday morning.

A great event is this arrival, you would think, if you could see the commotion among the owners of the nondescript trains we have before alluded to, as they rush forward to try their powers of persuasion upon our unsuspecting fellow-pilgrims who are bound for Sydney or Baddeck.

About four o'clock in the afternoon, we come in sight of grimy Pictou, and the next morning we wake up within sight of Charlottetown, the terminus of our steamer's route.

On Prince Edward Island we remain two days, and have plenty of time for a fishing trip among the trout brooks, and for a sight of the life of the islanders.

Then, if time or inclination forbids a longer stay in the provinces, we can take our steamer again Thursday night, and retrace our steps as we came, reaching Boston the next Monday morning.

The expenses of such a vacation are about as follows: —

Fare to Charlottetown, including state-room,	$12.00
" from " " "	12.00
Meals (breakfast and supper at 50 cts., dinner at 75 cts.),	15.75
Expenses in port,	10.25
Total,	$50.00

Thus we have a delightful excursion of nine days, and a sea voyage of more than half the distance to Europe.

VACATION ADVERTISEMENTS.

WHITE MOUNTAIN HOUSE.

ROUNSEVELL & COLBURN, Proprietors.

CARROLL, N. H.

Board, $2.50 per Day. Reasonable Terms by the Week.

This well known resort for Summer Tourists has recently been enlarged and refitted, and is now open to the travelling public.

Situated on the Ammonoosuc. Boston, Concord, and Montreal Railroad Station in front of house. Our rooms are comfortable, and furnished with new beds and bedding. Satisfaction guaranteed to our guests. We take pleasure in referring to our former patrons. We intend to make this house a HOME for those who visit the Mountains.

A GOOD LIVERY connected with the house.

We will take our patrons to all points of interest about the Mountains on reasonable terms.

TABLE OF DISTANCES.

B. C. & M. RAILROAD STATION	At the Door.
WILLEY HOUSE	8 Miles.
WAUMBEK HOUSE	11 "
CRAWFORD NOTCH	5 "
MT. WASHINGTON RAILROAD STATION	7 "
AMMONOOSUC FALLS	3 "
FABYAN HOUSE	¾ "

The tables will be supplied with the luxuries of the season, prepared by experienced cooks, and served by attentive waiters.

A share of patronage solicited.

The facilities for reaching this house are much improved by the extension of the Boston, Concord and Montreal Railroad to the door. From this house all points are easy of access, being centrally located among the Mountains.

ESTES AND LAURIAT'S PUBLICATIONS.

Warehouse 143 Washington St., Boston.

OVER 100,000 COPIES OF THIS WORK HAVE BEEN SOLD IN FRENCH.

Guizot's Popular History of France.

TRANSLATED BY ROBERT BLACK.

This great Work is now offered to the American public, and the Publishers, having spared no pains or expense in its reproduction, confidently believe that, as a specimen of book-making, it is unexcelled by ANY BOOK MADE IN AMERICA. By a special arrangement with the European publishers, we have secured Electrotypes of ALL OF THE ORIGINAL WOOD CUTS, by the celebrated artist, A. DE NEUVILLE, thereby securing impressions of the same fully equal to the originals. These Three Hundred Illustrations are pronounced by some of the best Art judges in the country to be the FINEST WOOD CUTS EVER PRINTED IN AMERICA. Besides the above, we shall add to the work FORTY MAGNIFICENT STEEL LINE ENGRAVINGS, by celebrated artists.

It will be issued in Semi-Monthly Parts, and the whole work will be comprised in NOT MORE than Forty-eight, nor less than Forty Parts.

Persons wanting a GOOD and RELIABLE History of France, need have no hesitation in subscribing for this, as it is the ONLY ONE of a popular nature, and by a STANDARD HISTORIAN, to be had in the English language. The Publishers offer it confidently believing that it will supply a long-felt want. The world-wide reputation of GUIZOT is a sufficient recommendation to the work, and a guarantee of its being a thoroughly correct and an intensely interesting history.

SOLD ONLY TO SUBSCRIBERS.

Fifty Cents per Part.

☞ Experienced Canvassers wanted for this magnificent work. Apply to the Publishers.

ESTES AND LAURIAT'S PUBLICATIONS.

Warehouse 143 Washington Street, Boston.

TESTIMONIALS.

Boston, Nov. 20, 1873.

Gentlemen: M. Guizot's History of France should be read by all who are not indifferent to historical studies. To a most interesting subject he brings the experience of a statesman, the study of a professor, and the charm of an accomplished writer. I am glad you are to place this recent work within the reach of all American readers.

Faithfully yours, CHARLES SUMNER.

Everything from the pen of Guizot is remarkable for thoroughness of investigation and exact statement. WENDELL PHILLIPS.

The work supplies a want which has long been felt, and it ought to be in the hands of all students of history. We cannot doubt that it will meet with the same favorable reception in England which has already attended its publication in France. LONDON TIMES.

The name of Guizot is a sufficient guarantee for the historical value of whatever he writes. E. G. ROBINSON, Pres. Brown University.

I should be glad to see Guizot's History of France in every school.
JOHN D. PHILBRICK, Sup't Public Schools, Boston.

The Popular History of France will be interesting, instructive, and worth to intelligent persons much more than it will cost.
W. A. STEARNS, Pres. Amherst College.

I have no hesitation in recommending this work.
JOHN W. BURGESS, Prof. History Amherst College.

There is no man more fit to write a History of France than M. Guizot.
JOSHUA L. CHAMBERLIN, President Bowdoin College.

We have seen no other subscription book which, for literary, artistic, and mechanical excellence, could be so unreservedly commended.
MICHIGAN TEACHER.

ESTES AND LAURIAT'S PUBLICATIONS.
Warehouse 143 Washington Street, Boston.

KNIGHT'S
Popular History of England.

As an appropriate companion to GUIZOT'S POPULAR HISTORY OF FRANCE, we have issued, in Eight Octavo Volumes, this truly magnificent work. It is an Illustrated History of Society and Government, from the earliest period to the year 1867. By CHARLES KNIGHT. With more than 1400 Illustrations, including 200 fine Steel Portraits.

This is the only complete Standard History of England.

The reader must go through Hume, Smollet, Macaulay, Froude, Martineau, and others, to go over the ground which is well covered in this work. Not only does it give with accuracy and system the historical events from the Druidical times down to the present decade, but it also depicts minutely the manners and customs of each era. The author suggests that its title should be a History of the English People, rather than a History of England. Numerous plates illustrate the text, and present vividly to the reader the actors and scenes of the narrative; and a copious Index facilitates reference to the contents of the work.

STYLES OF BINDING.

8 Vols.	8vo.	*Cloth, uncut,*	$25.00
"	"	*Cloth, beveled, gilt extra, trimmed edges,*	25.00
"	"	*Half calf extra,*	45.00
"	"	*Half Morocco extra,*	45.00
"	"	*Full tree calf, London bound,*	60.00

ESTES AND LAURIAT'S PUBLICATIONS.
Warehouse 143 Washington St., Boston.

KNIGHT'S HISTORY OF ENGLAND.

TESTIMONIALS.

We very cordially recommend these volumes to the readers whom they seek. We know of no History of England so free from prejudice; so thoroughly honest and impartial; so stored with facts, fancies, and illustrations; and therefore none so well adapted for school or college as this. — *London Athenæum.*

Its literary merits are of a very high order; indeed, nothing has ever appeared superior, if anything has been published equal, to the account of the state of commerce, government, and society at different periods. — *Lord Brougham.*

In Charles Knight's admirably comprehensive History of England, no topic that concerns the history of the English people has been omitted; the book of Mr. Knight being, let us say here, by the way, the BEST HISTORY extant, not only for, but also of, the people. — *Charles Dickens.*

Mr. Knight's book well deserves its name; it will be emphatically popular, and it will gain its popularity by genuine merit. It is as good a book of the kind as ever was written. — *Westminster Review.*

The best history extant, not only for, but also of, the people. — *All the Year Round.*

A standard book on the shelves of all libraries. — *London Spectator.*

The last and greatest literary work of his life. This history will remain, for many a long day, a standard work. — *London Times.*

This work is the very best History of England that we possess. — *London Standard.*

ESTES AND LAURIAT'S PUBLICATIONS.
Warehouse 143 Washington Street, Boston.

Elena.

By L. N. COMYN, Author of "Atherstone Priory," "Ellice," &c. 1 vol. 12mo. $1.50.

An Italian story of great power and beauty; one that is sure to live. — *Leeds Mercury.*

"Elena" is one of the most elegant and interesting fictions of the season. — *London Messenger.*

A very pleasing and touching story. It is sure to be read. — *London Daily News.*

Waiting-Hoping.

A Novel, from the French of ANDRE LEO. By J. E. GALE. 12mo. Cloth. $1.50.

The American Naturalist.

An Illustrated Repertory of Natural History. Making a compact library of popular papers on nearly every branch of this interesting science. 6 vols. 8vo. Cloth. $5.00 per vol.

Hogarth's Works.

Quarto. Cloth. With 62 full-page Plates, and descriptive letter-press. "A marvel of cheapness." $3.50.

The Rhine.

A Tour from Paris to Mayence, by the Way of Aix-la-Chapelle. With an Account of its Legends, Antiquities, and important Historical Events. By VICTOR HUGO. 12mo. Cloth. $2.50.

Chimes for Childhood.

A Collection of Songs for Little Folks. With 20 Illustrations by BIRKET FOSTER, MILLAIS, and others. Tinted paper, 208 pages. Cloth, 75 cts.; half bound, 60 cts.

ESTES AND LAURIAT'S PUBLICATIONS.
Warehouse 143 Washington Street, Boston.

Packard's Guide to the Study of Insects.

Being a popular Introduction to the Study of Entomology, and a Treatise on Injurious and Beneficial Insects; with Descriptions and Accounts of the Habits of Insects, their Transformations, Development, and Classification. 15 full-page Plates, and 670 Cuts in the Text, embracing 1260 Figures of American Insects. Sixth edition. 1 vol. 8vo. Price reduced to $5.00.

This book is now acknowledged to be *the standard*, and is used in the leading universities and institutions of Europe and America.

Half Hours with Insects.

A popular Account of their Habits, Modes of Life, &c. To be published in 12 parts, fully illustrated. Each part 25 cents. By A. S. PACKARD, JR., of the Peabody Academy of Science. The subjects treated are — Insects of the Garden, of the Plant House, of our Ponds and Brooks; Population of an Apple Tree; Insects of the Forest, as Musicians and Mimics; as Architects; Insects in Societies; The Reasoning Powers of Insects.

Say's Entomology.

A Description of the Insects of North America. By THOMAS SAY. With 54 full-page steel-plate Illustrations, engraved and colored from nature. Edited by J. L. LE CONTE. With a Memoir by GEO. ORD. Two vols. 8vo. Cloth, $15.00; half calf, $20.00.

This standard work is now out of print, the plates having been destroyed. We offer the balance of the edition at the above prices. It will soon become scarce, and command a very much higher price.

Our Common Insects.

A popular Account of the more common Insects of our Country, embracing chapters on Bees and their Parasites, Moths, Flies, Mosquitos, Beetles, &c.; while a Calendar will give a general Account of the more common Injurious and Beneficial Insects, and their Time of Appearance, Habits, &c. 200 pages. Profusely Illustrated. Price $2.50.

VACATION ADVERTISEMENTS.

ARRANGEMENT FOR 1874.

INTERNATIONAL STEAMSHIP COMPANY.

LINE OF STEAMERS BETWEEN

BOSTON,
PORTLAND,
EASTPORT, and
ST. JOHN, N. B.,

WITH CONNECTIONS TO

CALAIS, ME., HALIFAX, N. S., CHARLOTTETOWN, P. E. I., &c.

The favorite, superior, sea-going steamers of this line,

NEW YORK,   **NEW BRUNSWICK,**

AND

CITY OF PORTLAND,

Leave end of Commercial Whf., Boston, at 8 A. M., and Railroad Whf., Portland, at 6 P. M., for Eastport and St. John, as follows:

In **April, May**, and to **June 15**, every Monday and Thursday.

From **June 15** and through **July, August**, and **September**, every Monday, Wednesday, and Friday.

In **October, November**, and **December**, every Monday and Thursday.

Passengers by the morning and noon trains of Eastern and Boston and Maine Railroads from Boston, can take the steamer at Portland at 6 P. M.

Passengers forwarded by connecting steamers and railroad lines to Calais and Houlton, Me.; St Andrews, Woodstock, Fredericton, and Shediac, N. B.; Amherst, Truro, New Glasgow, Pictou, Digby, Annapolis, Kentville, Windsor, Liverpool, and Halifax, N. S.; Summerside and Charlottetown, P. E. I.

Rates of fare from Boston to Eastport, $5.00; Calais, $5.50; St. John, $5.50; Digby, $7.00; Annapolis, $7.50; Kentville, $8.50; Halifax, via Annapolis, Windsor, &c., $9.50; Halifax, all rail, from St. John, $11.00; Shediac, $8.25; Summerside, $9.50; Charlottetown, $10.50.

☞ *Through Tickets and State Rooms secured at the Agents' Offices, or of Clerks on board.*

AGENTS: A. R. STUBBS, Portland; GEORGE HAVES, Eastport; H. W CHISHOLM, St. John.

W. H. KILBY,
End of Commercial Wharf, BOSTON,

VACATION ADVERTISEMENTS.

THE NEW
MONTREAL AND BOSTON AIR LINE

NOW RUN

TWO FAST EXPRESS TRAINS, of new and elegant Cars, provided with all the Modern Improvements,

FROM

BOSTON to MONTREAL,

Without Change.

No Route from Boston presents such magnificent scenery. Passengers by this line travel through the

PARADISE OF THIS CONTINENT.

A most charming Panorama of River, Mountain, and Lake Scenery, including the grand views of **Lake Winnepesaukee**, **White Mountain Range**, and **Chrystal Lake**, will entertain the traveller for a distance of 250 miles.

☞ WE OFFER TO THE PUBLIC A LIST OF **TOURIST** AND **EXCURSION TICKETS** NEVER BEFORE SHOWN.

LEVE & CLARK, Ticket Agents,
94 *Washington Street, Boston.*

N. P. LOVERING, JR., Gen'l Ticket Ag't, LYNDONVILLE, VT. | GUSTAVE LEVE, Pass'r Ag't for N. E., 94 WASHINGTON STREET.

VACATION ADVERTISEMENTS.

Weekly Line

FOR

HALIFAX, PORT HAWKESBURY, PICTOU, and CHARLOTTETOWN, P. E. I.

Carrying the U. S. Mail.

THE STEAMSHIPS

CARROLL and ALHAMBRA

Will leave for the above ports alternately

Every Saturday, at 12 M.

No Freight received after 10 A. M. on day of sailing.
Shippers must send with Receipts the value of Goods for Master's Manifest.
For Freight or Passage apply to

WM. H. RING, 18 T. Wharf,
or E. H. ADAMS, 82 Washington Street.

F. NICKERSON, & CO., Agents.

VACATION ADVERTISEMENTS.

THE

CENTRAL VERMONT R. R. LINE

IS THE

Shortest, Quickest, and Best

ROUTE BETWEEN

New England and Canada.

EQUIPPED WITH *Pullman Cars*, AND ALL THE

MODERN IMPROVEMENTS.

☞ Send for the "SUMMER EXCURSIONIST" (a new ☞ edition each year) before you select your Vacation ☞ Trip or Summer Jaunt.

It contains several thousand excursions, including all the popular resorts, and arranged to meet the wants of the public as regards expense and time.

Tickets and full information obtained at

No. 65 Washington Street, Boston,

T. EDWARD BOND, Ticket Ag't.

L. MILLIS, Gen'l Supt. Traffic. S. W. CUMMINGS, Pass'r Agent.

ST. ALBANS, VT.

VACATION ADVERTISEMENTS.

Sea-Shore Route

TO

NORTH CONWAY and the WHITE MOUNTAINS,

AND

Only All-Rail and Stage Route

TO

RANGLEYS, MOOSEHEAD LAKE, and MOUNT DESERT.

Also, the All-Rail Route to the Maritime Provinces is via the

EASTERN & MAINE CENTRAL R. R. LINE.

Connections are also made at Portland with the Railroad and Steamboat Lines to all parts of Canada, Coast of Maine, and Maritime Provinces.

For further information, Time Tables, also to secure your Tickets, Berths and Chairs in the Pullman Cars, apply at the

GENERAL PASSENGER OFFICE:

No. 134 Washington Street,

BOSTON, MASS.

CHAS. F. HATCH,
Gen'l Manager.

GEO. F. FIELD,
Gen'l Pass'r Ag't.

VACATION ADVERTISEMENTS.

R. M. YALE,

SAIL-MAKER,

AND MANUFACTURER OF

ITALIAN AWNINGS, TENTS,

FLAGS, WAGON COVERINGS,

SACKINGS and STORE AWNINGS,

OF EVERY DESCRIPTION.

Cor. Commercial and South Market Streets,

(ENTRANCE 2 SOUTH MARKET ST.)

BOSTON.

R. M. Y. keeps constantly on hand a good assortment of Awning Stripes, of various patterns, and all orders will be promptly attended to. Also, Tents of all sizes, and Flags of all Nations, to be let on reasonable terms.

VACATION ADVERTISEMENTS.

BOSTON & MAINE and GRAND TRUNK R. R.

Boston and Montreal.

Passengers from Boston and the South and West will find that this **new route**, as now open, combines **comfort** and **convenience** with **cheapness** and **despatch**.

PARLOR AND
Pullman Palace Sleeping Cars

ON ALL THROUGH TRAINS.

☞ THROUGH TICKETS to MONTREAL, and all Intermediate Points, for sale at Stations on BOSTON & MAINE R, R.
☞ Baggage Checked Through FREE from REVENUE INSPECTION.

The BOSTON & MAINE RAILROAD also connects at Portland with the *Maine Central Railroad* for BATH, HALLOWELL, AUGUSTA, LEWISTON, WATERVILLE, BANGOR, EASTPORT, and ST. JOHN; with the *New England and Nova Scotia Steamship Co.* for HALIFAX; and with the *Portland and Ogdensburg Railroad* for **North Conway** and the **White Mountains.**

The road to ALTON BAY, WOLFBORO', and CENTRE HABBOR, and the Steamer on Lake Winnipiseogee, are owned by the Boston and Maine Railroad, and *Trains connect at Dover for these points with all trains on the main line.* The only *direct route* to WELLS, OLD ORCHARD, and SCARBORO' BEACHES, points which are UNSURPASSED for *good hotels, beautiful drives*, and *fine sea bathing.*

STATION IN BOSTON:

HAYMARKET SQ., at the Head of Washington St.

JAS. T. FURBER, Gen'l Sup't.

NEW AND IMPORTANT BOOKS

LATELY PUBLISHED BY

ESTES & LAURIAT,

Publishers, Booksellers, and Importers,

143 WASHINGTON STREET,

VACATION ADVERTISEMENTS.

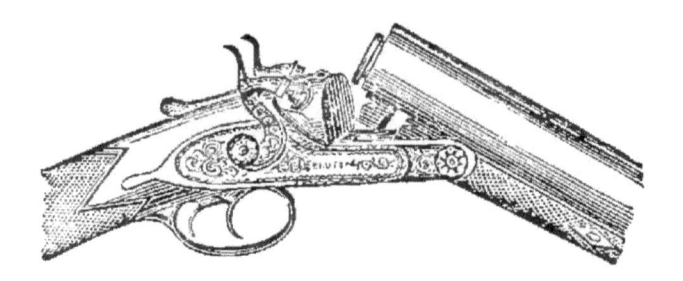

WM. READ & SONS,

13 Faneuil Hall Square, Boston,

DEALERS IN

FINE GUNS,

Both Breech and Muzzle-Loading,

Of all the best makers, "SCOTT," "WESTLEY RICHARDS," "MOORE," "WEBLEY," "GREENER," "ELLIS," and others.

AGENTS FOR

"W. & C. SCOTT & SON'S"

Celebrated Breech Loaders.

SCOTT'S ILLUSTRATED WORK ON BREECH-LOADERS, 25 cents, by mail.

ALSO

FINE TROUT AND SALMON RODS,

FLIES, REELS, LINES,

And everything in Fishing-Tackle Outfits.

TOURISTS' KNAPSACKS, &c., &c.

BALLARD'S, MAYNARD'S, WESSON'S, STEVENS', and WINCHESTER'S

SPORTING RIFLES,

Of all Calibres.

☞ Send for Circulars.